MW00512866

Praise for Alisha Rai's
Cabin Fever

"Cabin Fever is a different sort of paranormal erotica. There are no fanged creatures with an allergy to the sun or furry critters that shift under the heat of the moon. Instead, magic is the mystical element, and I have to say, it's a welcome change. ...The story is wonderful and the twists are unexpected. You'll be wondering who shot Alex throughout and will be shocked to discover who is responsible."

~ *Whipped Cream Erotic Romance*

"Cabin Fever is hot enough to melt snow and endearing enough to pull at your heartstrings. ...Combine vivid descriptions, good suspense and a touching love affair placed in the backdrop of the snowy West Virginia woods and you have a recipe for a great erotic novel. I'll be sure to keep my eye out for more stories from Alisha Rai in the future."

~ *Fallen Angel Reviews*

Look for these titles by
Alisha Rai

Now Available:

Glutton for Pleasure

Veiled Series
Veiled Desire (Book 1)
Veiled Seduction (Book 2)

Cabin Fever

Alisha Rai

A Samhain Publishing, Ltd. publication.

Samhain Publishing, Ltd.
577 Mulberry Street, Suite 1520
Macon, GA 31201
www.samhainpublishing.com

Cabin Fever
Copyright © 2010 by Alisha Rai
Print ISBN: 978-1-60504-769-0
Digital ISBN: 978-1-60504-753-9

Editing by Natalie Winters
Cover by Sasha Knight

This book is a work of fiction. The names, characters, places, and incidents are products of the writer's imagination or have been used fictitiously and are not to be construed as real. Any resemblance to persons, living or dead, actual events, locale or organizations is entirely coincidental.

All Rights Are Reserved. No part of this book may be used or reproduced in any manner whatsoever without written permission, except in the case of brief quotations embodied in critical articles and reviews.

First Samhain Publishing, Ltd. electronic publication: September 2009
First Samhain Publishing, Ltd. print publication: July 2010

Dedication

Special thanks to Rachel Nilles and Liza O'Connor, the poor saps who have been reading this manuscript practically from the time I scribbled it onto a napkin, and patiently answered questions like: should my heroine carry a handgun or a shotgun? The answer, of course, is both.

Chapter One

Her bedside drawer emitted only a whisper when she slid it open to remove the loaded .22 caliber handgun. Genevieve Boden cocked and raised the weapon in a smooth motion as she sat up, ready to fire even before her eyes could adjust to the darkness in her cabin. She held her breath and strained her ears, picking apart the normal nighttime sounds of her home and the forest in search of the unfamiliar.

Though she listened for it, the thump from outside shot a pulse of adrenaline through her veins and made her flinch. *An animal*, she told herself, as she slipped from the warm bed on silent feet. Strays often showed up on her doorstep. The reassurance didn't do much to ease the knot of tension twisted in her gut.

She reached the front door to hear another thump, louder than the first, and then a scratching noise, as if claws raked against the plank floor outside.

A big animal. With long nails?

A moan resonated through the house, launching goose bumps all over her skin.

Yeah, right. She couldn't think of any animal that sounded like that. Not of the four-legged variety, at least.

Genevieve kept the gun ready and knelt next to the front window. A trickle of sweat snaked down her spine as she twitched aside the curtain and peered out.

At first she could see nothing out of the ordinary, but then the tiny sliver of visible moon managed to do its job and a lump on the steps of her porch separated from the shadows. She squinted. Correction, a very large, still lump.

She reached up to hit the switch to activate the outdoor light.

Genevieve inhaled sharply.

The glow of the single bulb wasn't much, but it illuminated the face of the unconscious stranger sprawled flat on his back.

Whole and hearty, this man's features would have been a gift from God, with his fiercely masculine beauty, a series of hard planes and rough angles. It was just too damn bad he looked as though he had tangled with the devil. An angry swollen knot, as big as her fist, took center stage on his forehead against a landscape of bruises and cuts, visible beneath the light dusting of snow on his face.

Genevieve stood and unlocked her deadbolts before she dragged her instinctive response to a halt. Men didn't just fall from the sky on a daily basis to land, literally, at her feet. The guy might very well be beaten up, but something was fishy. Where had he come from?

Occasionally, she might stumble across a camper, but rarely in late November when the West Virginia mountain nights were so cold. The first snow of the season had started to fall earlier that day, and there were already a few solid inches lying on the ground. Even in good weather, her home was quite a hike for a healthy person to make on foot from the nearest town. If the roads were still in drivable condition, a car could get you pretty close, but she didn't see any horse or car in the darkness of her yard.

She nibbled her lip and watched the man, counting the

seconds he lay there without moving. She got to twenty before she gave up, cursed her conscience and opened the door a crack.

"Hey. Mister." She hardened her tone, careful to keep the gun pointed in his direction and her finger on the trigger. When there was no response, she opened the door wider and leaned out. "You okay?"

The man moaned and she jumped, her hand tightening on the weapon. His eyelids fluttered open and his head turned toward her movement. He focused on her, his black eyes commanding despite the supplication in his hoarse one-word plea. "Help."

Self-preservation warred with the desire to help. Undecided, Genevieve stood her ground while he flattened his hand against the plank floor and struggled to rise. He managed to heave himself further onto the porch before collapsing on his back again. The meager pool of light spilled over his upper body, revealing a dark stain over the shoulder of his shredded jacket.

Holy crap, that's a lot of blood! Horror trumped her caution, and she hurried out to kneel beside him, laying the pistol within her reach. His jacket was light and completely inappropriate for the weather. Genevieve fumbled for a minute with the zipper, and then just gripped both sides of the material and ripped it apart. When she spread the windbreaker open she got her explanation for the state of his outerwear. The man must have torn the lining out with his hands to wrap a wad of material around his shoulder. The light blue nylon had turned dark red.

The knot was difficult to undo, but it finally came apart. The material actually stuck to his skin. Luckily, she wasn't given to squeamishness, or peeling it off would have made her gag. The rip in his tan shirt was convenient, and she stuck her fingers in it to make it wider. She drew in a startled breath at the sight of his torn flesh below.

The jagged hole in his shoulder left little doubt he had met the wrong side of a gun. He flinched when she probed her fingers underneath him, but the quick inspection told her the bullet had gone clean through. That was the only good news, though. An unhealthy combination of dried blood, dirt, insect bites and scratches caked it, and the skin around the jagged edges of the injury was purple and puffy with infection. Now that she was close enough to feel the heat radiating off him, she realized his half-open eyes were too bright with fever. "When were you injured?"

His mouth worked. "Two—days? Don't remember. Saw your smoke..."

Two days? He'd been crawling around the cold woods with a serious wound for a couple of days? No wonder he was so bad off. She'd heard of a guy who got shot while stranded outdoors once and died of infection within seventy-two hours. This man was lucky he hadn't also been attacked by animals or succumbed to dehydration.

The mystery as to his lightweight jacket was solved though. Weather turned quickly in the mountains. A couple of days ago, or even yesterday, the windbreaker would have been more than sufficient. Had he stayed out all night tonight, he would have frozen to death. "Who did this to you?"

"Don't know...tried to get police..." The man shook his head, dazed. "Lost my phone."

Phone. Yes. Why hadn't she thought of that? No police, never, but she could get help. "Stay here." As if he could go anywhere.

Leaving him down for the count, she palmed her gun and

darted into her cabin. After Mom had died, she'd broken down and bought the telephone hanging on her kitchen wall.

By the time she got to the second digit in the closest hospital's number, though, Genevieve realized she wasn't hearing any telltale beeps. "Fuck, fuck, fuck." She slammed it down into the cradle and picked it up again. No dial tone. Dead. What a time for one of her few modern conveniences to fail her.

Genevieve returned to the porch and studied the stranger for a second. Though she knew nothing would happen, she tried to slow her racing mind and focus past the man's physical plane.

Nope, nothing. No colors, no energy bouncing around his body. To think, auras had once been as visible to her as someone's nose.

The cold bit through her nightgown, and she shivered, wondering how he had managed to make it without dying. Who was he? A vacationer? Ski season had just begun, though the nearest resort was a ways off. Perhaps a winter fisherman? He had said he tried to get help...would the bad guy have tried to call the cops? *Have you forgotten who the cops are here?* Genevieve shook off that thought. She couldn't in good conscience just leave the guy on her doorstep to die a painful death. Besides, she was tougher than she looked and he was in no shape to do any lasting damage to her. "We need to get you in the house. Can you walk that far?"

He grimaced and managed to raise his upper body a few inches. She kept her gun in one hand and slung his left arm over her shoulders to pull him upwards, using every ounce of will to help him to his feet and inside.

He was a big man, at least a foot taller and roped with heavy muscle. Despite the strength that came from working her small farm, she huffed and puffed by the time they cleared the doorway. She lowered him to a sitting position against the wall closed the door and turned all four deadbolts. Genevieve switched the safety on the gun and placed it on her counter before stoking the fire and pulling the mattress and bedding from her queen-sized bed in the corner to create a pallet in front of the fireplace.

"Come on, now." Genevieve helped her unexpected guest toward the mattress. The few steps into the cabin must have tired him. He leaned on her more heavily, and little trickles of sweat beaded along his hairline by the time he lay on his back. Though the fever raged through his body, his eyelashes were crusted with ice, his lips blue. She needed to see to his wounds before she could really bundle him up.

She gathered her supplies from under her bed, as well as water and towels, and hurried to his side. One of his shoes was missing, the other ripped, as if an animal had gnawed on it— hmm, maybe he had come across some four-legged predator after all. The jacket and casual tan button-down were a lost cause, so she wasted no time in using her kitchen shears to cut them right off. The jeans gave her a bit of pause, but she made a split-second decision to destroy those as well, instead of taking the time to try to work the wet denim off his dead weight. When he wore only his boxers, she surveyed him from head to toe with a clinical eye.

The scratches and bruises all over his body and the giant knot on his noggin weren't great news, but the most worrisome injury was the mess on his right shoulder. Had it been taken care of right away, it probably wouldn't have been a serious wound, but she'd never seen anything quite as bad as the putrid infection that had set in. She cleaned the wound and the skin first, wincing along with him as she unstuck the dried blood and grime from hair and flesh. After the cleansing, she gently probed the area around the wound.

"Angel?"

His labored breathing turned the question into a soft whisper of sound. He had a slight accent, a hint of New York clipping the words. She glanced at his face. His eyes were slits of coal, his brow creased with pain.

She made her smile reassuring, her voice brisk. "No angels here. My name's Genevieve. What's yours?" She tried to work fast as she distracted him.

"Alex—oh, God." He gritted his teeth when she covered the infected area with an antiseptic rinse before packing a poultice with herbs and tying it tight over his wound with a bandage.

She stuck a straw into the glass of water, bringing it to his parched lips. "Alex, you need to drink, okay?"

He gave a tiny nod in acceptance. She raised his head and supported him until she judged him to have had enough.

"Gen—Angel. Gonna die?" he gasped as she put the drink down.

He deserved honesty. "I don't know."

"Will you...tell my mom? My brother. I love them."

She swallowed. "Yes. What's your full name?"

He didn't seem to hear her, his gaze turning inward. "Don't wanna die."

"I'll do everything I can," she whispered.

"Beautiful..." He closed his eyes and slipped into unconsciousness.

Despite her assurance, she honestly did not know if she could promise him life. Forget the dehydration and exposure—she had no way of knowing what damage the bullet had done internally, and the flesh was even more infected than she first believed. Her gut tightened in anxiety. She had worked automatically, calling on everything she had ever read or been taught, but the sad truth was, she had no practical experience with gunshot wounds. However, at this point, she wasn't certain he would live until she could get him medical care.

Genevieve studied his fitful rest. His chest rose and fell far too shallowly.

I love them.

I'll do everything I can.

Not for the first time in three years, she mourned her lost power. Healing had once been as natural to her as breathing. She'd saved countless animals in her childhood and adolescence. Granted, she'd never tried to cure massive infection before, but now she couldn't even attempt it.

Or could she? She couldn't, in good conscience, let him die if she had the ability to save him.

She laid her trembling hand flat over his bandage, closed her eyes and willed her mind and body to relax.

Nothing.

She clenched her eyes tighter, so frustrated a bit of moisture leaked out. Not tears; she never cried, damn it.

Mom, if you have any pull up there...please just help me out. I'm not hurting this time, I'm helping. Let me just...oh.

Energy slammed into her body, and she felt rather like she'd been plucked from her small cabin and thrown into a dark closet. The world receded around her and became condensed to the man in front of her and then only to his pain. Trying to think past the euphoria that came from having her lifelong power returned to her, she pictured the purple and blue flesh beneath the bandage, and punctured it in her mind, allowing the pus and bacteria inside to pour out down his arm. The man growled in agony.

The pus still trickled when she focused her energy into the

wound itself and visualized repairing ripped muscle and flesh, fusing the torn sides together. His body bowed in an arch. He tipped his head back and roared in pain as he heated to a boiling point. A wet sheen of sweat covered his body and face. The power surged into him, and he glowed purple for just an instant.

In the space of a breath, it was finished. She doubled over, the pain in her shoulder and head blocking any other sensation.

Christ, it hurt. She'd forgotten how much. His pain, magnified by three...oh, it hurt. Genevieve whimpered and curled onto her side. *Breathe.*

She lost track of how long she lay there, unable to think beyond the pain. A half an hour? One hour?

When she could lift her eyelids without flinching, she knew the worst was over. Sweat covered her face, her nightgown stuck to her body, but she was able to move. Though her limbs felt heavy with exhaustion, she rallied her remaining strength to finish what needed to be done. She removed Alex's blood-and-pus-soaked bandage, scrubbing his body with a wet towel, drying with another. Drying sweat would be the last thing he wanted when he went through the next stage.

He was barely conscious, grooves of pain and suffering carved around his mouth. *I feel you, buddy.* The lines of strain deepened as small shivers coursed through his body. Genevieve finished drying his legs and feet and ran to her small closet to get extra blankets. By the time she'd rushed back to him, his shivers had grown to great racking shudders. "Cold," he rasped. "So—cold..."

She knelt next to him, working as fast as she could to bury him under the mound of blankets. A bright red flush covered his entire form, a reaction to the power she'd crammed into his body. His core temperature had taken a hard hit, to go from close to freezing to burning hot in the space of a couple of minutes.

The shudders didn't dissipate, and Genevieve grew worried. She gave a startled squeak when a hot hand reached out from under the blanket and grabbed her wrist. "Need you," he bit out. She was startled enough that she did not protest as he drew her under the blankets with him.

He heaved over onto his uninjured side, his face buried into the crook of her neck, hot breaths gusting against the sensitive skin. His heavy leg pinned her. His right hand shifted on her belly, and she spared a moment of worry that he would aggravate his shoulder by jostling it even the slightest bit. It didn't seem to matter to him, though. Perhaps what she had done had numbed his body, or his brain was so far gone with pain and fever, a little more hurt didn't affect him. His rough hand smoothed down her body and over her hip, catching in the fine lawn of her cotton nightgown. He grasped it before she realized what he was doing, dragging it up her body until it bunched above her breasts. Genevieve gasped as he pressed their naked bodies together, one large hand coming to rest under the curve of her breast, the other anchoring in her long braid. As his flesh met hers, his shudders finally subsided and he slipped fully into unconsciousness, his body turning into a dead weight.

He was so heavy, and her home was warm to begin with, so his furnace-like body temperature didn't help. She shifted just a bit, but froze when the rough hair on his chest abraded her nipples. Would it be possible to get out from under him without moving? She wedged a hand between them to gingerly rest it on his hot chest and gave a slight push, but he remained immobile. She must be tired, she decided, if she was able to notice the resilient, muscular flesh beneath her palm. *Shame on you. He's near death.*

Shaking her head, Genevieve pushed harder. He grunted and moved, enough for her to slide her upper body out from underneath him. She shoved her nightgown down until it covered her to at least her upper thighs.

She should move, get the gun, and keep watch on this guy. Try out her old, decrepit radio and see if she could contact someone for help. He could be some sort of career criminal, the bad guy. Genevieve yawned loudly instead. God, she was tired. Maybe she could take just a minute to catch her breath. Then she'd get up. Her state of exhaustion was related to him, so it wasn't like he would be particularly spry in attacking her if she stayed for a second.

She craned her neck back a bit to study the stranger's face. When the Lord saw fit to drop a man on her doorstep, He didn't do it by half measures. This was a Man with a capital letter, the kind who probably choked people with a cloud of testosterone. Beneath bruises and cuts she knew were already healing at ridiculous speeds, the stranger's face was perfectly formed, with a strong, straight nose, high cheekbones and full sensuous lips.

His skin was a toasty shade of brown. He was Hispanic, she guessed, which was unusual in the mostly Caucasian surrounding communities. She followed along his tanned throat to what she could see of the rest of his body, feeling a tiny twinge of guilt for ogling him while he slept. The twinge got swept away in admiration. His shoulders were broad, his stomach a flat washboard. A dark sprinkling of hair covered his chest, narrowing to a line that disappeared into his boxers. His left hand still lay on her stomach and no amount of calling herself foolish could stop her from noting he wore no wedding ring, had no pale strip of skin on his ring finger.

With her defenses lowered by utter fatigue, she wasn't able

to stop the impulse that had her stroking back the dark lock of hair that fell over his forehead. She lingered, exploring the coarse and curling strands.

His eyes popped open and caught her in the act of fondling his hair. "Sorry," she whispered, embarrassed, and lowered her hand. His impossibly long lashes drifted closed again, but not before he tightened his hold and pulled her toward him. He gave a satisfied grunt when she pressed against his entire length.

His heat permeated her body. Sleep sucked at her consciousness, and she tried her best to fight it. *Get up, get the gun. You can't just snuggle next to this guy.*

She couldn't trust him, but surely he'd be out for a while. It wouldn't hurt to give in to her heavy eyelids for a few minutes, right? Just for a bit. Five minutes tops, and then she'd be back in fighting form.

Roll out of bed and doze on the ground, then. She gave a halfhearted jerk to move away, but his fingers caught in her braid. Her exhausted mind gave a shrug, and she couldn't even pry her eyes open anymore anyway. Sleep rushed over her like a Mack truck. Her last conscious thought was the groggy realization that she hadn't had a man on top of her in years. Alex was a definite upgrade.

Chapter Two

Being dead hurt. Why hadn't the priests or nuns who'd taught at his elementary school ever talked about that?

Apparently, being dead also meant you went blind, because he couldn't see anything except an inky blackness. Well, that sucked.

No, he wasn't blind, he realized a split second later. His eyes just wouldn't cooperate and open. Shit, someone had sewn them shut. His heartbeat accelerated, his breathing soughing in and out of his lungs. Would he have to spend eternity like this?

Calm down, Alejandro.

Papa. Alex relaxed. Okay, if he was hearing his late father's voice again, which he hadn't heard since he was twelve, then he must be dead. Maybe that's what those hours of pain and torture and crawling in the freezing godforsaken mountainous forest had been all about. His father had been whispering to him then, too, in bursts of Spanglish, he recalled woozily. Urging him to keep going, to get to the cabin. He could see it, a tiny little log thing carved out of the wilderness. He could even recall the angel who had greeted him, though she was a bit hazy. The impression of soft arms and a backlit face stayed with him. Maybe everyone who died went through the same journey. Like some metaphorical shit.

Fuck, he probably shouldn't be swearing in Heaven.

But if he was in Heaven, why did he *hurt*? His body felt like a massive collection of bruises and cuts. It even hurt to breathe, though did you still need to breathe when you were dead? His right shoulder and arm were the most affected, but his head wasn't in too good a shape either.

Could he be in Hell? No. He was toasty warm, but it was a comfortable warmth, not a fire-and-brimstone heat. Besides, he'd done some stuff he wasn't proud of, but he hadn't been that bad, and his father wouldn't be with him if he was. Carlos Rivera had been too fine a man to end up in Hell. Purgatory then? That would explain the pain.

Since he couldn't open his eyes, he put all of his effort into trying to move his arms. He froze when his hand slipped over something large and soft.

His fingers twitched on the softness. He didn't need anyone to tell him he was cradling a breast. All straight men loved breasts, but Alex *loved* breasts. God, this was a gorgeous one. He could tell without even seeing it. Large, pillowy, with a long tight nipple jutting against the cotton fabric that sadly covered the mound. D, maybe even DD, he guessed.

If there was a breast in bed with him, Alex figured there was probably a woman to go along with it. The lure of being able to see her popped his eyes open.

He slammed them shut again when light stung his pupils. Very slowly, he inched them back open, trying to adjust them a little at a time.

Weak sunlight lit the room, creeping in from the curtained-off windows. Alex turned his head and caught his breath, the pain in his body receding. An angel indeed.

She had a face that he'd only seen in the Botticelli paintings an ex-girlfriend had dragged him to see at the Met once. Soft and round, the chin a sweet curve. Her lips were full and naturally pink, her skin a blemish-free expanse of ivory and roses. Her eyes were a startling shade of violet, tipped with long black lashes.

Wait, her eyes? Yes, they were open, staring back at him. They held that silent gaze for a while, neither of them speaking.

When the tension became too high for him, he swallowed his mouthful of cotton. "Dead?" he croaked.

"No. But if you don't move your hand, you may be."

His ears were too busy soaking in the rich cadence of her voice to comprehend her. She had a slight drawl that softened and dragged out her syllables and made him think of hot summer nights and cold sweet tea. When he did finally allow the words to sink in, he wanted to jump for joy and whimper with despair. No, he wasn't dead. Why did he have to move his hand? His hand liked where it was. His hand was very happy.

However, he hadn't been brought up to molest strange women, and since this wasn't a very sexually permissive Heaven, he had to abide by the rules of polite society. With a great deal of effort, he released the piece of happiness in his grip and shifted his body.

Agony promptly pierced through his right side. Christ, he hadn't felt like this since that time last year he'd been...shot. He'd been shot. His brow furrowed, but that caused even more streaks of pain to radiate through his body.

A soft hand slid under his neck, propping up his head. Something cold touched his lips, liquid trickling down his chin. It felt so good he opened his mouth automatically. After a second, he began to gulp, the icy water a relief to his dry and parched throat.

He must have drained the glass because the water stopped coming out, and he was gently lowered back to the pillow. The cool hand passed over his forehead and he turned his head toward it, despite the nagging pain it caused his head. The woman withdrew her hand and he almost cried out for her to return, as if he were a little boy in need of his mommy.

Unconsciousness tugged at his brain, but he fought it long enough to watch her walk away. Her long hair was as black as his own, but it swung in a braid all the way down to her hips, strands sneaking out as if they were too wild to be contained. The sun had risen; more light pierced the room. It surrounded her body in a glowing nimbus, and when she turned in profile, it slipped right through the cotton of her loose gown, highlighting her body.

Like a complete pussy, his breath caught in his throat. Christ, this was a *woman*. The palm that had been cradling her breast tingled. He wanted her back, only skin to skin so he could feel her nipple and the texture of her flesh. Her hips were wide, the thighs plump. He could see the curve of her belly and he wanted to nuzzle it, lick it, nip at it. Her ass would overflow his hands. He was so affected that despite his lack of general well-being, his cock twitched where it lay soft against his thigh. The slight response thrilled his woozy brain—it proved, more than anything, that he was alive.

"You're so beautiful." His words were a croak, but she must have heard because she looked over her shoulder, violet eyes wide and startled. Something clicked into his brain.

You are hers. Take care of her.

Yes, mine.

As he fell asleep, he couldn't help but thank God he was alive, plus a little extra fervent gratitude. *Lord, I'll take another gunshot. Just don't let this woman get away before I'm well.*

Chapter Three

Genevieve laid her knitting on her lap, right over the barrel of her gun, and stretched. She relaxed back into the softness of her late mother's favorite armchair and picked up the two needles again, though she had no real desire to work on the sweater. She just figured it was easier to keep her hands busy and occupied.

Thinking of her hands led to thinking of his hands. Or more specifically, where his hands had been yesterday.

She felt more than a little shame at how long she'd lain motionless as his hand had roved over her body before oh-so-spectacularly squeezing her breast. Logic dictated she should have moved away from the guy as soon as she was conscious. She blamed her punch-drunk state. It wasn't like she'd instigated it or enjoyed it. After all, what did she know about him? That underneath all of his injuries, he was a devastatingly handsome man?

Genevieve snorted. Yup, that's all she knew about him.

Certain her powers had returned, she'd given herself a headache yesterday staring at his sleeping body. A person's aura wasn't really as woo-woo as so-called psychics made it out to be. Everybody had them, a slight electromagnetic field surrounding the body. Calling it science made her feel less weird.

When Genevieve had been a child, she'd stared at every person she'd come into contact with, mesmerized by the shifting colors. By the time she'd reached ten or so, she'd managed to adjust her brain to where she could choose when and where she was able to view it.

It wasn't like reading a person's mind, but over the years with the help of her similarly afflicted mother, she'd learned to comprehend the layers of colors. Genevieve had always figured it was a kind of trade-off for making the women of her family so bizarre. Worried who to trust? Concerned about that neighbor with a pitchfork and noose? Here's this handy-dandy color chart for the good guys!

The method had a scary accuracy at pinpointing basic personality and emotions. Also, since her particular skill lay in healing, she could tweak certain aspects of the aura to speed good health along. As she'd learned, tragically, she could also do the opposite.

Genevieve shook her head. Maybe that's why she'd been given only part of her powers back. Perhaps she was deemed too dangerous by whatever cosmos or deity dealt with freaks like her.

In any case, not only did she not have any way of ascertaining Alex's personality or intentions—except waiting for him to wake up and then trusting whatever he told her, which seemed like a dangerous thing for someone who had issues to begin with—but she couldn't even help his healing further along.

Genevieve couldn't lie; she was worried. She'd certainly never tried to fix someone as badly injured as Alex had been, and her powers had been on a three-year leave of absence. What if she had screwed his body up somewhere inside? Alex had barely stirred over the course of an entire day and night.

not even when she'd changed his bandage or forced some water down his throat.

The only thing she was hopeful about was the fact his various wounds did seem to be mending. In the meantime, she was going stir-crazy, clutching her gun and refusing to sleep, terrified she would wake up with a criminal choking her.

With a sigh, she left her chair and walked over to her phone, already knowing the line would be silent when she picked it up. Yup, nothing. It had never been out for this long. Then again, she hadn't tested it through a record snowfall. The lone fuzzy station coming through her battery-operated radio had confirmed that this was no little hiccup. What had been a few flurries the night she found him had turned into a massive dump of the white stuff that showed no signs of stopping any time soon. Normally, that wouldn't be a big deal, since she kept plenty of food and firewood on hand, and her backup generator would keep the heat on in case her power went down.

Of course, normally she didn't have an ill man lying on her ground. Even if her ham radio had been functional, calling for help would be futile. The plows were busy shoveling out the more populated areas before hitting the isolated rural region she lived in. Likewise, even if she did still own a car, she couldn't bundle the guy up and take him down blocked roads.

Genevieve exhaled in a rough sigh. The snow had never bothered her before. She loved tromping around her land in her boots. Unfortunately, her common sense had rejected that idea. She'd gone out once yesterday, rushing to the barn to feed her horse and chickens before sprinting back inside.

Alex probably hadn't shot himself. So there was at least one other person out there with a gun. Granted, it would be tough to make it up to her place right now, but who knew when and where Alex had gotten hurt? By the extent of his injuries, it was quite possible he had been in the woods for a couple of days, as he said. However, it didn't take much to get turned around in these trees. He could have been crawling around for a day or so within a one-mile radius.

She walked over to the window and peered outside into the winter wonderland, straining to see any movement in the trees, a knot of tension and resentment in her belly. Damn it, this was her world. Nobody should dare threaten it. Not again.

Her breathing accelerated faster than she could control it and Genevieve inhaled and exhaled, long and slow, until it steadied, despising the fear and helplessness she had not felt in so many years.

Damn the man and damn her conscience for being unable to stay uninvolved. He stirred behind her. Attuned to his movement, she spun around, but he was only settling into the mattress on the floor. Lucky guy. One night dozing in her chair and she'd kill for her plush mattress. Despite her guilt-induced bare trappings, she appreciated her little luxuries.

She couldn't wait till he woke up so they could really have a chat. So far his only words had been variations of the same as he gazed at her as if she were a work of art: *beautiful, pretty* and one very mumbled *sweet.*

She snorted. Yeah, right. Not that she felt bad about her body, but she was realistic. In high school, she realized that she'd had the full three strikes against her: her mother and the fact they lived way out here, rumors of their bizarre powers and her weight. She'd been home-schooled for elementary school and middle school, too, so perhaps that was a fourth strike.

When she'd attended the University of West Virginia, she'd received her first taste of life away from a canopy of suspicion, and her self-confidence had grown a little at least. She'd had a few boyfriends, two who turned into lovers, one worth remembering: a sweet, normal guy named Billy, and they'd continued their relationship after they'd graduated. It had fizzled out and they'd parted amicably. In fact, Genevieve considered Billy one of her best friends. Though he lived two hours away, he'd come down to visit her a few times and called her regularly, though he was obviously puzzled as to why she'd dropped her life and moved back to her rural home three years ago. Particularly since her mother had been dead for two of those years.

Genevieve shook off that thought and concentrated on the man in front of her now. Her first impression had been accurate. He looked like he'd been fashioned to tempt good women into sin. All that tawny skin, the dark coloring, bulging muscles and a full lower lip that just begged to be nibbled...

She inhaled and glanced away. *Bad Genevieve.* Case in point, a man who tempted her—rational and pragmatic Genevieve—to sink her teeth into his body when he was lying on her bed unconscious, was definitely not a man who would fall in lust with her at first sight. Men who looked like him were invariably attracted to equally muscular and toned blonde bombshells. She was none of the above. Though working the small farm kept her healthy, she loved to eat, and she'd gained more weight since she'd lived here alone in the past couple of years. Sometimes in the winter all she could do was sit around and munch.

Speaking of which, she was starved. She shot her half-naked invalid another look before she carried her gun with her over to the fridge and propped it up against the counter. She was more at ease with the shotgun so she'd stowed the handgun away in her drawer. Did she really think the guy was going to be able to jump out of bed and grab her? No. But it made her feel more in control of the entire situation to have a weapon directly on hand.

Alex awoke to the finest scents in the world: bacon, coffee and woman.

God, he still hurt, the kind of hurt that went down to the bone. Oddly enough, though, he felt light years better than he had the last time he'd tried this. How long had he been drifting in and out of consciousness? Weeks?

As awareness returned to his mind, he nestled into the softness of the mattress beneath him, half afraid to open his eyes. What if his mystery woman had left? Or worse, never existed? What if he turned his head and found out that he was really just lying in some hospital or his old bedroom back at his mother's Westchester home?

He rejected that idea. The woman was his lifeline. He didn't remember much of what had happened to him, but seeing her had bolstered his will to live, he was certain.

Having learned his lesson, he opened his eyes in small increments. The curtains on the windows were tied back, flooding the room with sunshine. The place was empty, and he felt deflated.

With the kind of practice that his job had honed, he took in the entire dwelling with a single glance. It was just one large rectangular room. His sharp eyes sought out the exits and noted with approval the amount of hardware on both the front and back door, which was partially open and looked as though it led to another room rather than the outdoors.

He lay in the middle of the room in front of the fireplace. The furnishings were sparse and utilitarian, with feminine touches here and there—a bright yellow rug on the floor, plaid curtains on the windows, a dented tin can filled with dried fall leaves on the table. A kitchenette with a small table, an old-fashioned refrigerator, stove and sink took up one corner and in the other lay a bedroom area, half hidden by a quilted curtain. No television or radio visible, but the bookshelf against the back wall was crammed with books, next to a comfortable armchair and floor lamp. Everything was neat and tidy, which appealed to him. He'd always been a stickler for clean lines and zero clutter.

A noise and a movement by the back door alerted him, and he lowered his eyelids to watch under his lashes as the woman entered the room. As she stepped into the sunshine, his heart accelerated.

He hadn't imagined her amazing body. Those full curves were showcased in a pair of jeans and a bright red sweater. Her loose hair reached her ass and curled against the upper curve. The soft waves swung shiny and full as she walked to the stove with a purposeful stride and picked up the spatula.

His cock jerked, as if to remind him it was there. *Down, boy. You're not running the show here.* Once again, though, he was gratified by the sign of life. If he was able to get turned on, surely he wasn't too bad off. He sighed.

At the noise, she jumped and spun around. The pan clattered to the burner, and her exotic violet eyes pinned him.

No, not violet, he realized. Blue. A deep blue, so rich and shifting it gave off the impression of purple fire.

Like a lovesick fool, he was so busy waxing poetic, he didn't notice her hand shooting to her side until an antique shotgun appeared clenched in her grasp.

So, his angel packed heat? She looked as if she knew what she was doing too, holding the gun like a pro.

Damn. She was hot.

He smiled despite the fact that the cuts on his face pulled and stung. "Hello." Unfortunately, instead of the seductive purr he had been hoping for, a harsh croak emerged. He licked his dry lips with an even more parched tongue and tried again. "Water?"

She hesitated, but with some tricky maneuvering managed to keep the shotgun on him while she fetched a glass from a cupboard and filled it in the sink. She grabbed a straw from a drawer and stuck it inside.

She stopped about an arm's length from where he lay and extended the glass to him. He tried to reach for it, but his hands were shaking so bad he couldn't quite get a grip.

With a distinctly un-angel-like sigh, she knelt next to his pallet. She cast him a suspicious look, and he attempted to appear as non-threatening as possible. In fact, laid out as he was, he wasn't sure how he could come off as threatening. She put the gun right next to her and held the straw to his lips. The moment the cool water hit his throat, he pulled harder at the straw, struggling to sit up to get closer to that wonderful feeling.

She placed her arm underneath his head to support him, and he almost moaned in pleasure. Her chest was close to his face, so close he could simply turn his head and rest it against her soft breasts. The last thing he wanted was for her to run away from him, though, so he refrained.

After the glass was drained, he waited for her to release him quickly. Instead, she slowly lowered his head until it rested on the pillow. She scooted back, picked up the gun and pointed it at him again.

He tried not to pant. He'd never realized he had such a thing for tough chicks.

He cleared his throat and tried to speak again. "Hello." Much better.

She licked her lips. "Hello. How do you feel?"

Like someone had run him over and then backed up to finish the job. His machismo decided to pick now to kick in, though. "Not too bad."

"Yeah?" She was staring at him so hard he thought she might go cross-eyed in a minute.

"Got...something on my face?" He tried to smile so she'd know he was teasing.

The woman shook her head, in frustration, it seemed. "Close your eyes."

Alex didn't take orders very well. Nonetheless, he didn't question her, since closing his eyes felt more than a little good. Her cool hand rested on his chest and he almost whimpered in relief.

And then...her hand wasn't cool anymore, but warm. Heat tingled throughout his entire body from his fingertips to his toes. Energy burned through him, until he felt like he could take on a mountain and win.

Stunned, he opened his eyes in time to find her dropping her hand from his chest. She swayed on her knees, catching herself on her palm on the ground. Her face was pale, the skin under her eyes bruised.

"Are you okay?" He felt much stronger than he had five minutes ago. No marathons yet, but he could speak without hurting now.

She waved a hand at him, breathing slow and measured. From experience, he knew she was trying to breathe through pain. Why did she suddenly look as sick as he had felt? What the hell had she done?

"Feeling better?" she bit out.

He focused on her. Easier to do that than consider the unexplainable. She seemed more stable now. "Yes. And you?"

She raised one finely arched eyebrow. "Always."

His mind was so muddled, it felt like he had dozens of

thoughts, all just out of reach. He grabbed for the most urgent. "I remember you."

"Do you?"

"My angel."

"I assure you, I'm no angel."

He wasn't going to argue with her. Despite all of her obvious fleshly charms, there was something a bit otherworldly about her. Combined with her oh-so-interesting little trick... "What's your name?"

She hesitated. "Genevieve."

Beautiful. It suited her, musical and soft. "Genevieve. I'm Alejandro—Alex."

"I know. You told me that first night. Don't even try to remember. You were out of it."

"Yes. Where am I?"

"My home."

He looked around the cabin. "Where is your home?"

"We're deep in Harrison Woods."

These woods were huge, miles and miles of unpaved roads and towering trees and mountains. More than a couple of the townspeople had warned him about wandering in, said they had a few hikers who got into trouble here in the past. And this one woman lived here? Surely she wasn't all alone? "How did I get here?"

Her tone hardened. "You showed up on my porch in pretty sorry shape. Why don't you tell me how you got there?"

"I have no idea."

She raised her brow. "Amnesia only works in soap operas."

He smiled. "I'm not claiming amnesia. What day is it?"

"Tuesday. I found you on Sunday."

Tuesday? Granted, his concept of time was a bit wonky, but two days of recovery to be feeling as good as he was now? "I don't understand...what did you do to save my life?"

"Just cleaned and bandaged you. When were you shot?"

Maybe he wasn't injured as bad as he'd thought. Maybe she'd used some herbal drugs on him. Maybe he'd imagined the way her touch had given him strength. "Friday. Afternoon. I noticed a dog on the side of the road. He looked injured, so I pulled over to see if I could do anything. He got spooked and limped into the forest so I followed."

"That was...very nice of you." She sounded surprised.

He tried to keep his chest from puffing out a bit. He didn't rescue animals to score points with pretty girls.

But he liked that it scored some points with Genevieve. "Anyway, next thing I know, bullets are flying all around me. I took a hit to the shoulder." Back in the old days, before his nerves had failed him, he would have reacted immediately and probably avoided getting shot. The sound of the first bullet in the quiet clearing had sent him into flashback mode, leaving him dangerously vulnerable. Thanks, post-traumatic stress disorder.

Since he didn't want to sound like a total wuss, he hurried to clarify. "That wouldn't have been that bad, if I hadn't fallen down and smacked my head against a tree. I passed out."

Her gaze drifted to the knot on his head. "Concussion."

"Probably. When I came to, the sun had set. I was so out of it, I guess I must have gotten turned around and crawled deeper into the woods." There was more to the story of course, but he didn't want to bore her with the gruesome details. Personally, he didn't care if he ever remembered how he'd managed to staunch the bleeding of his shoulder and keep moving in the wild all while combating the horrible nausea,

35

dizziness and unconsciousness his concussion had brought about. At least he could add "sucking on tree bark for water" to his resume, though. Small comfort.

"You don't know who shot you?"

He shrugged. "There's been a lot of talk about poachers in that area. That's my best guess. All I know is, the person either didn't see me or spooked and ran when they saw me lying there." No need to tell her about his suspicion that the shooter had been following him after he had regained consciousness. The injuries must have made him paranoid. His job, since he'd moved to Bumfuck, West Virginia, consisted of very little excitement; just a lot of paper pushing and thumb twiddling.

The shooting had come from out of nowhere, and he truly believed it was the result of an unscrupulous hunter. Couldn't have been premeditated. No way could anyone have known he would stop by the side of the road that day. "Accident or not, though, I'm pissed as hell. Some people shouldn't be allowed to have a firearm."

She pursed her lips. "I thought you sounded like a *damn liberal.*"

He would have snorted with a laugh if he knew it wouldn't hurt so much. Her deadpan tone was a perfect mimic of some of the more conservative townspeople. "I have no problem with people having guns if they know how to treat them properly and if they have a need for them—say, if they live in the middle of nowhere by themselves. Like you, right?"

Her lips twitched before her eyes narrowed in suspicion. "Why do you ask that?"

Oh, shit, he shouldn't have asked such a personal question. He could practically see red flags going up in her brain. *Way to go putting her at ease. Why don't you ask her if anyone's going to miss her if she vanishes too?* "No reason. Just wondering. Anyway, I can't wait to get my hands on the prick who shot me."

"Might be a while."

"It's only been a couple of days, you said."

"Yeah, well, paved roads are a bit of a luxury out here, and currently they're all snowed out."

"Snowed out? There wasn't a flurry in the sky when I stopped on the side of that road."

"Yeah, you were lucky. One more night outside, and you would have been dead. Temperatures change quickly in this area." She gestured to the window. "It hasn't let up since I found you."

His mind instantly jumped to his poor mother and brother. If he'd been reported as missing, which, after three days of absence from work, he'd assume he was, they'd be frantic with worry. "Do you have a phone? Did you call for help?"

"No. Well, I do, but it seems to be out. Otherwise I would have tried to get you to a hospital before the roads snowed out. I've been checking it periodically, but no luck yet. The power's been flickering in and out, but I have a generator, so that's not that big of a deal."

If you'd gone to a hospital, you'd be dead. The thought popped up in his mind. He didn't know why he was so certain, but he was. Genevieve had been able to save him when modern medicine probably would have given up on his sorry ass. "My family's going to be worried sick."

For the first time, her eyes softened. Her hand relaxed on the gun. "I'm sorry about that. I have an old ham radio, but unless you know more about fixing electronics than I do, I'm afraid it's inoperable. If the phone isn't working by the time the snow lets up, though, I can use my horse or dirt bike to get help. In the meantime, I'm afraid you're pretty much stuck at this resort with me."

All in all, not a bad prospect. In fact, if he didn't know his mother was probably crying hysterically over her rosary at this very minute, he wouldn't mind the forced vacation with this pretty woman at all. He didn't remember much of his fevered dreams during the past couple of days, but he knew she'd been his rock through the hellish nightmare. "Well, at least the scenery is nice."

She blinked. "Are you flirting with me?"

Alex grinned. He loved a direct woman, and Genevieve seemed upfront to the point of rudeness. "Yes. Why, is there a Mr. Hermit I should be worried about?"

She smiled back, and his heart skipped a beat. He'd heard of that happening, but Lord, it was a funny feeling. "No."

"Me neither. I mean, I'm not married. No girlfriend. Or kids. Not that I don't like them. Love kids." He tried to clamp his mouth shut. He'd never been a smooth Latin lover, but he could hold his own in the flirtation arena normally. Something about her called out to the blushing fourteen-year-old in him, crazy over his first crush.

She was staring at him. "That's...nice."

"Sorry, I'm rambling. My brain's still a little messed up."

"It's okay. So, were you vacationing around here or something? It's kind of late in the season for tourists." The admission of his weakness appeared to have relaxed her even more, because she settled onto the hardwood floor next to his bed. Her expression wasn't exactly as soft and sweet as he would have liked, but the suspicion seemed to have eased.

"No, I live down here."

If he hadn't been watching her so closely, he would have missed the stiffening of her body. "You don't sound like you're from around here. Besides, I've never seen you before. It's a small county."

"Brooklyn, born and raised. But I moved down here about three months ago."

She was watching him with alarm. "You...you don't know who I am?"

"Except for the woman who saved my life? No. Should I?"

"You must live in Newbury, then."

She was referring to the larger, more cosmopolitan town a little farther south. "Nope. Harrison."

There was no subtlety in her response this time. She physically withdrew from him.

"You really haven't been there long then," she said with no inflection. "Or you would have heard of me."

Alex tried to figure out the new vibes in the room. Fear? Defiance? "Your reputation is so grand, then?"

Her eyes were hooded. "I wouldn't call it grand."

"Actually, I'm kind of pissed no one told me a young woman lived out here all alone. It's a little too far for regular patrols, but it's still under our jurisdiction."

"Patrols?"

He shook his head and extended his hand, a bit ashamed to see the slight tremor in it. "We really need to introduce ourselves. What's your last name?"

"Boden."

"Genevieve Boden, meet Alex Rivera. I was just hired on as the new chief of police."

If he'd thought the title would ease her misgivings about having a strange man who'd been shot lying in her house, he was dead wrong. He might as well have said he had become the new serial killer in town. Her face leached of color, and she stared at him with legitimate horror in her eyes. He reached for her arm in concern, but she crawled backwards.

"Are you okay?"

She swallowed. "Bainsworth finally retired?" Her voice was carefully casual, but the fear and worry in her eyes belied her tone.

"He died. Cancer." Alex paused when he noticed her infinitesimal flinch. "I'm surprised you didn't hear. It was almost four months ago. The position was open, and the council was desperate. Frankly, I think they just wanted some fresh blood in here." He eyed her curiously. "I take it you didn't like the previous chief very much."

She gave a short, high laugh and stood. "I need to get breakfast together." Her face, tight and hard, discouraged conversation. He much preferred her with her mouth soft and her face flushed. Actually, he preferred her best naked and writhing underneath him.

It looked as though he would need to work some serious sweet talking before that happened.

Well, hell.

Chapter Four

The new chief of police.

She'd saved the life of the new police chief. Oh, the irony.

She didn't know why she'd convinced herself he couldn't possibly live in Harrison. Maybe it was because she knew everyone who lived there and no one new ever moved to that damned place. Granted, she stayed far away from them, but she tried to keep up with what was going on in town. Why, the last time she'd spoken to Ron White, one of her mother's only real friends...

Had been well before the summer. So Bainsworth hadn't died yet, and the gossip on the exciting new hire wouldn't have existed then. Since the rest of the townspeople and her avoided each other like the plague, she wouldn't have gotten the news any other way. Newbury, where she went for all of her supplies and necessities, was far enough away and large enough not to bother with the rumor mill of its nearby neighbors.

Genevieve felt like throwing a good old-fashioned tantrum. In some weird corner of her mind, she'd entertained the notion she'd claimed a part of Alex when she'd saved his life. She didn't want him tainted with the ugly brush she used to paint the residents of Harrison.

Not only a resident, but the police chief...ugh. Her irrational fear of lawmen was a bit ridiculous, she got it. Alex wasn't Bainsworth, but still, he was a somebody, a man of influence and power. Men of influence and power plus small towns which looked the other way plus isolated women equaled nothing but disaster.

Should have let him die. Genevieve rejected the thought as soon as it occurred to her. No, she was grateful her powers had returned long enough for her to help Alex.

Now she had to do some severe damage control, though. She couldn't let word get back that she wasn't the wicked witch of the woods. Her reputation was part of her protection.

While she picked at her breakfast at the kitchen table, she tried to think of what to do with her troublesome houseguest. Oddly enough, the fact he was from New York reassured her a bit. There were people in the small mountain town of Harrison who considered residents who lived there for ten years "outsiders". If he'd lived here a couple of months, then it wasn't likely he was in any inner circle of corruption. Still, she couldn't trust him, could she?

She'd helped him prop his head up on his pillows before handing him his food. He had cast a mournful glance at the bacon and eggs on her plate, but accepted his bowl of almost-liquid oatmeal. Despite his clear preference, he had methodically eaten his way through two bowls before breaking the silence with a decidedly casual tone. "Are you an international jewel thief?"

"I beg your pardon?"

"Just wondering why you hate cops."

"What makes you think I hate cops?" she hedged.

"Oh, I don't know. Maybe it's the way you hung all those do-not-touch signs all over yourself as soon as I mentioned my occupation."

"What are you talking about?"

"You pointed a gun at me."

"I pointed a gun at you before you told me you were a cop."

He started to speak, but then stopped and looked thoughtful. "Huh. You're right. Still, before, it was like a friendly gun pointing. You got all icy after. If you'd picked up the gun then, it would have been a mean, scared gun pointing."

"A friendly... You're crazy. And I don't hate all cops." Just those who abused the system, the ones within the good-old-boy hierarchy who could get away with murder.

"You can tell me."

She shot him an exasperated look. "Stop it."

"Did you rob a casino?"

"Eat your breakfast."

"This isn't a breakfast. This is what the nuns served us in elementary school."

"I'll be sure to give your complaints to the chef."

He grinned, his teeth very white against his brown skin. "I wasn't complaining. Just correcting."

He was damn charming when he was conscious. Then again, he'd been so charming when he was unconscious, she'd decided to snuggle up against him and fall asleep in his arms.

She tried to ignore him as she swallowed the bacon that settled like lumps in her stomach. When his bowl thunked onto the ground, she looked up in alarm. He lay against the pillows, his skin ashen below his natural color. His eyes were closed, the black lashes heavy fans against his cheekbones.

"You okay?"

He shook his head the slightest degree. "Tired."

Well, sure he was tired. She felt the tiniest pang of remorse for grilling him unmercifully as soon as his eyes were open. The tiniest.

His breathing evened out and she continued to watch him. "So far, you haven't been the best of houseguests." Of its own accord, her mind spun an erotic fantasy about a handsome stranger who stumbled onto her porch. They would have wild monkey sex right away and then...

Alex snored.

She stared at him with a twinge of wry humor. Why was reality so complicated?

She studied the bandage on his shoulder, spotted with a couple drops of blood. Genevieve figured she should take advantage of his sleep to change the gauze. It would be easier to handle touching him if he wasn't awake, easier to keep her distance. The cuts and bruises on his face were healing by the minute, revealing an even more attractive man. The white blankets had fallen when he'd sat up that little bit. They rode low on his hips, the snowy color highlighting his cut, naturally tanned abdomen.

The large bandage marred the beautiful landscape. She fetched her supplies, water and towels. As she unstuck the bandage from the wound, she did enough wincing for both of them. Genevieve dipped the washcloth in water and wiped away the blood and pus that had leaked under the gauze. She wrung the cloth out and grabbed a fresh towel, following the path the previous cloth had taken. Her vanity was more than pleased with the sight that greeted her. The torn flesh hadn't completely fused together, not yet, but the red and angry edges looked a damn sight better than they had before.

She laid her hand directly on top of the wound, closed her eyes and directed another flow of energy into the healing flesh. When she opened her eyes, the skin along the jagged edges flared purple for an instant and then subsided to a pink that looked even better than it had before. She smiled in satisfaction, so proud she wanted to pick him up and stick him to the fridge. *I did that! Me, me, me.* The rebound she felt was only mild, a slight dizziness. Either she was getting better, or he didn't need much help.

Don't get too cocky, Genevieve. She sobered at the recollection of her mother's voice. Yes, she would cool it. No one knew better than her what happened when a person became arrogant and careless with what they'd been given.

She cast a quick glance at his face before she took the washcloth to his chest. She kept her motions efficient and practical when she really wanted to drag the towel slowly over his delineated muscles. Not even the many scars riddling his body could detract from the work of art that lay in front of her. She knew the explanation behind the newer ones, but she had a sudden desire to pepper him with questions about the others, like the big healed scar on his thigh. She had no right to any kind of information, but while she was touching him, and they were all alone, it was tough to remember that.

Yesterday she'd cleaned him more personally, even removing his boxers, laundering them and dressing him again. Somehow, though, this seemed far more intimate.

It was because he was no longer just a piece of meat, a generic male lying on the ground. He'd woken up and talked to her and looked at her with those beautiful black eyes and... Genevieve sighed.

"Why are you sad?"

His voice made her hand jerk, and she realized she'd simply rested it over his navel. Thank God the wet towel had been between their skin. His voice was rough, and she plopped the towel in the basin and grabbed the glass of water she'd meant for him to drink before he fell asleep. No IVs here, and he wouldn't want to be dehydrated.

He drank, finished the glass and laid his head back down. "Why are you sad?"

"I'm not sad. I was just changing your bandage."

They both looked down at the drying wetness on his abdomen. Far from the site of his wound. The skin around his eyes crinkled as he looked back at her. Her face flushed and she tried not to sound defensive. "You don't want to smell sweaty, do you?"

"Nope. You can sponge bathe me if you like."

His tone was low and brought all sorts of erotic thoughts to mind. She cleared her throat. "I did it yesterday. You should be fine now until you can do it on your own."

"You sponge bathed me yesterday?"

"Well, I couldn't just let you lay there all dirty, now could I?" Shoot, there went her vow not to sound defensive.

"Of course not. Thank you."

"Anyway, I'm done. Let me just bind you up again." She looked up in time to see his confused frown as he studied his gunshot wound. Uh-oh.

"What the fuck? I don't see any stitches."

"I didn't use any."

"You should be able to see even a Steri-Strip."

She stroked a cloth along the injury to dry any wetness. His muscles contracted. "Really?"

"I was shot *four* days ago. There was a hole in my shoulder. I felt it when I was trying to staunch the blood. So where the fuck did that hole go, Genevieve?"

"You went from thanking me to yelling at me? And they call women temperamental."

She watched as he visibly tried to control his temper. "I'm sorry I raised my voice. I'm just trying to understand how you made a bullet wound practically disappear overnight."

Right, 'cause then he could run back to town and tell people what she could do. She'd have every Tom, Dick and Harry on her doorstep, looking for a cure for their sprained ankle and headache. "Just used some herbs my mom taught me about."

"No way herbs brought about this kind of healing. I know a little something about injuries. I want to know what you really did."

"What could I possibly have done, except use medicine and cleanliness?" she asked mildly.

"I don't know." He glanced up at her, his eyes unreadable. "Maybe you're a witch. Maybe you have some sort of healing power."

With every word he spoke, she could envision the hordes of people who would start creeping around her precious hideout. She forced a laugh. "Nice one. Do you know how crazy that sounds?"

"I've seen some crazy stuff. And I remember things, from after you found me, about my body burning—"

"You were feverish."

His jaw set stubbornly. "There's no way I could be this far along in my recovery unless you did something funny. The injury barely hurts."

Genevieve dropped the towel at her side and stroked over the edge of the wound. Then she pressed down at just the right angle.

He inhaled. "Oh, fu—okay, okay. Let go."

She increased the pressure the tiniest bit and blinked at

him. "What?"

He grimaced. "So it's not completely healed. I get it. Stop."

Good enough. She ducked her head and tried to hide the slight smile playing on her lips.

When she looked up, he was studying the old shotgun leaning against the kitchen cabinet. His expression was serious as he glanced back at her. "You know how to use it?"

Genevieve snorted. "I can probably outshoot you."

Alex's eyes twinkled. "Them's fightin' words, sweetheart."

She rolled her eyes and pressed a fresh bandage over his wound. He arched his back, making it easier for her to wrap it around him. She didn't realize how much she had to lean over him until she felt his breath on her neck.

Genevieve sat back and finished tying the bandage. "Are you thirsty?"

He suddenly looked uncomfortable. "Actually..."

"Yes?" she prompted when he trailed off.

"I—that is, I kind of need to, you know, use the bathroom. Do you have indoor plumbing?"

Genevieve cast him an exasperated glance. "Of course I do."

"Just checking. Okay. Point me in the right direction."

"You can't get up!" She rested her hand against his chest. "I'll get you a bedpan."

The tips of his ears turned red. "I am not pissing in bed. If my injury looks as good as it does, I can get up and walk."

"Your head was hit pretty badly."

"I'm sure you rubbed whatever super-mushroom you used on my head as well."

"Okay. Fine." She pressed her hands against his chest. "If you can push against me and get up, I'll let you use the toilet."

He smiled grimly. It was clear that he was none too pleased that she was requiring the test, but he needed to stay prone for another day, at the very least.

If she could supply energy to heal, she could take it away without it adversely affecting her. *Let's see if you still remember how to do this.*

Of course, he'd know for sure after this that she wasn't normal. However, it was far better if he viewed her gifts negatively instead of positively. If her reputation as the creepy witch of the woods suffered, she'd have no protection.

Her hand heated, recapturing the little boost she'd offered him earlier.

When he pushed up against her, she had no trouble pressing back. Apparently, she'd given him even more than she realized. His body flinched and he collapsed against the mattress. Tiny beads of sweat popped out on his brow. He grimaced in pain. "What the fuck?"

She kept her hands on his chest and opened the door in her mind, pouring the fission of energy back into his body. The pain receded from his expression. Despite the way her head spun from the back and forth, it couldn't have happened fast enough for her. There had been no joy in delivering that hurt to him.

It took her a couple of minutes to compose herself before she could look him in the eye. The anger was expected, a strong man's response to having his pride compromised, but the shadow of fear just about punched her soul. "What are you?"

Her body stilled. Each beat of her heart sounded like cymbals crashing in her head. What, not who. Damn him to hell.

She was what they had made her. Him and his cronies.

Not him, reason interjected. *Anyway, you should be happy.*

This is what you wanted.

Whatever. She allowed a mask of indifference to slip over her features. "I'm the little girl who just pinned a big bad cop to the bed. Looks like you'll be using a bedpan."

"Genevieve..."

She didn't want to hear him. If it wouldn't have looked childish, she would have pressed her hands over her ears and hummed.

Instead, she went through the back door to the room that had been added on to her home. The large closet in there held the nursing supplies her mother had been forced to use at the end of her life. She fetched what she needed and returned to Alex. "Look at that, it's pink too. Bet you'll love that." She placed the pan next to him and did her best to walk casually to the front door. "Have fun."

"Wait, where are you going?"

She jammed her feet into a pair of boots and swung her coat off the coatrack. "Sorry. I've got other bodies depending on me too. See you later."

"Genevieve! Genevieve, damn it, get back—"

The snick of her door cut off his tirade. A grim smile crossed her face as she envisioned him swearing at the door and then struggling to use the bedpan on his own.

What, indeed.

Chapter Five

Genevieve expected to return to a barrage of insults and a bed full of angry male. Instead, Alex was dead asleep. He didn't even stir when she crept close to take care of his bedpan. Nursing her mother for as long as she had, the chore was just that to her, a chore.

She was still irritated with the guy, but her outrage had burned off as she stomped in the snow outside. To be fair, she had wanted him to look at her like that—she'd deliberately done something which would take his pride away and instill fear. He'd be wary of her now, keep his distance. No more of that bantering and flirtation.

Alex needed his rest so badly. She slipped out to the back room. It had been fashioned as a sunroom with a large closet on one end and a small bathroom at the other. A huge bag filled with her crafts took up one end of the beaten-up couch. She settled into the cushions and removed a half-finished blanket. She entered her crafting Zen mode. The silence in the small cabin was broken only by the sounds of the house settling, the wind rustling and the click of her needles. From her position, she watched the afternoon slip away, the darkness of night overtaking the darkness of a snowy afternoon. She snapped on the small lamp next to her.

When the sky had become pitch black, the falling snowflakes only visible thanks to the light from inside, Genevieve heard a slight stirring coming from within the main cabin. She laid down the thick blanket and made her way inside.

Sure enough, Alex was struggling to sit up. Just as she was about to help him, he managed to haul himself up on the pile of pillows. When he noticed her, his gaze was still a little blurry. With the short strands of his hair sticking up and the stubble on his jaw, he should have looked crazy, not sexy. She waited for him to stare at her in horror, or call for her to be burned at the stake. Instead, he rubbed his hand over his face. "Did I fall asleep?"

"For most of the day." She waited. Now. Now he would start looking for a pitchfork.

He shook his head. "I didn't mean to. Is it still snowing?"

"You needed the sleep. And yes. Phone's still out too."

"I guess I did need it. I'm still tired."

What game was he playing? Were they going to pretend she hadn't messed around with his body? Well, that kind of didn't surprise her. Most people repressed what they couldn't explain. He'd convinced himself, no doubt, that it had been a figment of his imagination. She didn't know if she was disappointed or elated, neither of which made sense.

"Genevieve."

She couldn't help but stiffen. *You shouldn't like the way he says your name.* "What?"

"I'm sorry."

She blinked. He was apologizing to her? "For what?"

"You know for what. I shouldn't have said what I did. It was wrong and cruel, and I apologize. Can you forgive me?"

Genevieve studied him, looking for the catch. What the hell? His gaze was direct, his expression open. Sincerity dripped off of him. She couldn't help but be suspicious. "What's your angle?"

"No angle. I was wrong."

She shrugged. "Fine."

"Seriously. You saved my life, and I paid you back by treating you like I was scared of you."

"You are scared of me." She meant for the words to be low and a bit threatening, not the plaintive statement it came out as.

His response was instantaneous. "No. I was pissed when you did what you did, though I get that it was for my own good. But I knew from the start something was extraordinary about you, so I wasn't completely blindsided. As I was lying here, my mind cleared and I was finally able to put all the pieces together."

Extraordinary? "I took your strength away. Do you get that?"

"After you gave it to me, right?"

Yeah, that was the only way she'd been able to weaken him without it hurting her. If she'd weakened or injured him on purpose, she would have been charged a greater price. Still, he shouldn't know that. "I've hurt people before. Your first reaction was right. Keep that in mind before you start romanticizing me."

"You won't hurt me."

"What makes you think that?"

"I trust you."

His words were so simple, they stunned her. "Why the hell would you go and do that?"

His brow furrowed. "I don't know. There's this...connection between us. Don't you feel it?"

Yes. Hell, yes. "So you're telling me on the basis of your...feelings...you're going to decide I'm a trustworthy person. Despite the fact that I can do stuff that isn't readily explainable. Is this how you do all your cop stuff?"

He smiled. "You mean, am I a naïve fool? I don't think so. But I'm willing to bet my life you couldn't hurt a fly."

She froze. "Don't."

"What?"

"Don't make that bet. You don't know what I've done."

He studied her, and his voice gentled, as if he were talking to a spooked animal. "Okay. How's this? I bet you couldn't hurt me. You saved me. You're a healer, aren't you? What else can you do?"

When she remained silent, he exhaled. "You don't trust me. I'm really just interested. You know, I'm a Hispanic mutt. My dad was Puerto Rican. Mother is Columbian, Brazilian and Costa Rican. Our culture lives and breathes supernatural stuff. You don't know how many stories I was told over the years about my grandmamma and my aunt. They were healers too."

A spike of interest rose. She'd never met anyone, outside of her own family, with legitimate powers. "Yeah?"

"Yes. They worked as midwives. My cousin, she still lives in Puerto Rico, carries on their work. Though I don't believe any of them are anywhere near as powerful as you are. They've certainly never saved anyone from a fatal injury."

The admiration in his gaze was so unexpected, she didn't quite know what to say. Nobody had ever accepted her. In high school she'd been the freak, in college and after she'd kept her abilities tightly under wraps, and when she'd moved back...well, that had effectively turned the people who'd considered her a freak into people who used her to scare their kiddies into behaving.

He must have mistaken her contemplation, for he lay back against the pillows and sighed. "Do it."

"What?"

"Do it again. Whatever you did before. Make me weak."

"What?"

"I want you to understand that I do not fear you or find you disgusting. I will never hurt you. I owe you everything, and I'm ready to swear on my father's grave I won't harm you. However, if you feel threatened or nervous around me—and don't tell me you're not wary of me—I give you full permission to make me weak again. Now or whenever."

She stared at him, stunned. The fact he was willing to voluntarily give up his strength, submit to her mercy, for no other reason than to make up for her hurt feelings and make her feel safe—her, a woman he barely knew—it was just unbelievable. She'd never heard of such a thing.

She didn't bother trying to see his aura. For the first time in her life, she wondered if she could trust someone from their words alone. "You mean that?"

"I would have died without you."

All right, that solemn, devoted look was a bit too much for her. "You're exaggerating. You weren't really that bad off. If you were, I wouldn't have been able to do a thing."

"So you *are* admitting you did something?"

What the hell. His little-boy eagerness was so damn endearing she could barely resist eating him up with a spoon. "Yeah. I'll admit it."

"That's...amazing. Have you ever done anything like this

before?"

"Not of this magnitude. Plus, my abilities have been on the blink for a few years."

"Think of what you could do for those who are suffering—"

"Stop right there." She held up her hand. "You said you owe me, right?"

A guarded look crossed his face. "Yes."

"I want to collect. I need your vow that you won't tell anyone else about me. You can tell them I'm fearsome, that I can kill men with a single look, but not about the rest of it."

"Why?"

She hesitated, but decided she could give him a little bit of the truth. "My safety depends on it. Right now, most people in your town fear me. They call me a witch and stay away. I've encouraged that for reasons of my own. If you blab that I'm pulling in strays and mending them, then I don't know who would come out here and try to hurt me."

His face darkened. "Nobody will hurt you."

"The best way to ensure that is for you to keep quiet about me. You can say you came across an abandoned cabin or whatever you want. Just don't mention me."

"Deal. Though I will not consider my debt paid, since this is such a small thing."

She rolled her eyes. "It's not a small thing to me."

"One thing though—I'd rather you not go outside. Especially if you make me weak like I was before. Whoever shot me could still be out there."

She stiffened. "You said it was a hunter."

"What's to stop an unscrupulous hunter from coming and poaching out here?"

Nothing. And if it was someone who wasn't familiar with her reputation...aww, fuck. "I'll do my best to stay inside," she allowed. She couldn't let the animals go hungry.

"Okay, then. Do it if you want."

She should have been thrilled at this opportunity. He'd be alive, still healing, but no threat at all to her, physically or emotionally. When the phone came back online, she could call someone out here to get him to a hospital to receive proper care. She'd be on her own, the way she liked it.

She couldn't do it, though. Couldn't emasculate him like that. No matter how much he unnerved her.

As she stared at him, it was like a switch flipped in her brain. He wasn't bluffing, which meant he trusted her enough to put himself at her mercy. Perhaps she could try trusting him back?

She hadn't trusted anyone in three years. What a novel feeling. He had given his word not to blab all over town about her and she believed him. He said he wouldn't hurt her, and she couldn't see him raising a hand to her. Was she being foolish? Maybe. But she liked this, liked the easiness and lack of worry that came from being able to let go of the constant fear. Honestly, Genevieve wasn't even sure she knew how to trust anymore. Maybe he'd been sent here for her to...relearn?

It was too much for her to think about all at once, the ideas overwhelming her. She broke their gaze and stood. "Are you hungry?"

"Genevieve..."

"Are. You. Hungry?"

"Please, yes."

She crossed to the fridge and pulled out the makings for dinner. Her stomach rumbled, reminding her that she hadn't eaten since breakfast either. "Do you like chicken?"

"Love it."

"Great. Just wrung this one's neck yesterday."

At his silence, she looked over her shoulder and slammed the fridge closed with her hip. "Is there a problem?"

He swallowed. "No. I wish you hadn't told me where that chicken came from, though."

"You mean this chicken?" She held up the meat in her hands. A little imp of mischief urged her on. "Sorry, does it bother you that I pick it up from the pen, grab its neck and twist it until it snaps?"

Alex closed his eyes. "Actually, I'm not hungry anymore."

"Where do you think meat comes from?"

"I think the meat fairy puts it in my grocery store."

She laughed, a bit startled. It had been a while since she'd heard herself laugh. "Sorry to disappoint. The meat fairy doesn't come out this far." She proceeded to put dinner together.

When she brought his bowl of broth over to him, he looked at it with dismay. "Are you punishing me?"

She wasn't that petty. Okay, she was, but she wasn't mad at him, so no, she wasn't punishing him. "You need to build your strength."

"I'll build it a lot easier if you give me real food."

"You can eat this, or nothing. Your choice."

He glared at her, but she had no intention of budging. Especially now that she had an inkling of what a marshmallow he was beneath his scary job and huge physique. Sure enough, when she started to turn around, bowl in hand, he breathed out a rough sigh. "Okay, fine. Give it to me."

Alex sat up on his own and took it from her with ill grace.

She returned to the stove and ladled some of the soup and chicken into her bowl. She ate standing over the sink. Blessedly, he didn't speak much, as if sensing her contemplative mood. When he was finished, she washed both of their dishes.

"You don't have any psychic powers, do you?"

She cast a startled glance over her shoulder. He spoke about her abilities with the same kind of casual tone someone would use to ask if she had blue eyes. "What? No. Why?"

"Guess I couldn't be that lucky. I was just thinking of how worried sick my mom must be. She's listed as my next of kin. I'm sure they called her when I didn't show up to work, if not the next day, then Monday for sure."

Her heart softened at the worry and concern in his voice. "You sound close to her."

"My dad died when I was twelve. She raised us by herself. It was hard enough to move down here when she was still in Westchester. I can't even imagine what she must be going through, thinking I'm lying somewhere dead."

"My mom raised me by herself too." The words slipped out before she could stop them.

He paused. "Yeah? Did your dad die too?"

"No. I never knew him." Genevieve wiped her hands on a towel and turned around. "I wish there was some way to get word down."

"Yeah, well. What can you do, right? Like I said, I've probably hit my quota for miracles this week. You know, with the gorgeous woman saving my life and all."

Her face flushed at the warmth and clear sexual interest in his tone and smile, but she disguised her flustered state with a toss of her head. She walked over to her small cupboard and pulled out a blanket.

"What are you doing?"

"I need a blanket. I have a couch out there. That's where I'll sleep." Their eyes met, and by the wicked glint in his eyes, Genevieve knew he must recall exactly where she'd slept that first night. To her relief, though, he didn't bring it up.

"You're going to bed?"

She shrugged. "I thought you might want to sleep. Figured I would read for a while."

"Could you read out here?" He grimaced. "I'm not tired, and I think I'll go crazy if I have to lie out here by myself. It's so damn quiet outside."

"City boy. You aren't used to the quiet?" Yet another difference between them. She loved the solitude.

Okay, so it got a bit trying sometimes. The pros outweighed the cons.

"Not at all."

It was a small enough concession to make. Honestly, she didn't want to leave his presence just yet. "Fine. Do you want something to read too?"

"I don't think I could concentrate. Could you read to me?"

"Um. I guess so. What would you like to read?" She tucked the blanket under her arm and went over to her bookshelf.

"Whatever you were planning on is fine."

She tossed a wry glance over her shoulder. "All of my new releases are romances. I doubt you'll be interested."

He shrugged. "That sounds fine. I like romances."

Genevieve snorted. The idea of this man's man reading a book with heaving bosoms on the cover was laughable at best. "Seriously?"

A corner of his mouth kicked up. "Are you kidding me? We didn't have *Playboys* lying around for me to discover as an adolescent—I got a nice education from the Harlequins my mom read." His brow wrinkled. "Though I do remember wondering why so many virgins appealed to Greek tycoons."

She laughed. That made twice now. If she didn't watch herself, she'd become downright jolly around him. "I think that's a question for the ages." She perused her latest stack of books and chose the least explicit-looking one. The last thing she needed to do was read him something erotic or sexy.

Genevieve stoked the fire and then sat cross-legged next to him. She opened the book but had a bit of trouble concentrating on the writing when he shifted to get comfortable. The firelight played over the muscles of his chest, and she was abruptly reminded of his nakedness below the sheet.

Get over it. Genevieve opened the book and began to read. Other than her voice, the room was silent except for their breathing and the crackle of the fire.

It was a peaceful feeling, and she slipped into the rhythm and pace of the story, everything fading around her until she became absorbed. She'd only read to her mother when she was sick, and she'd forgotten how much she enjoyed it.

When the log gave a particularly loud crack, she jumped, pulled out of the book. She was surprised to note how many chapters she'd read, that her throat was hoarse. She looked down at Alex, certain he'd fallen asleep.

Instead, his gaze was direct on hers, wide and unblinking. "Are you tired?" he rumbled.

She shook her head.

"Why did you stop?"

Could a voice be intimate? He used that tone, that low, deep tone, and Genevieve felt like he'd reached out and nibbled on her neck. "My throat hurts."

He shifted. "Maybe we should stop for tonight then."

Stop for tonight. As if they had endless nights to pick the story up. She closed the book.

"You have a beautiful voice. I could listen to it for hours."

Had she thought he sounded intimate before? He'd gone straight from kissing her neck to stroking between her legs with that little statement. "Thanks." She started to get up but was startled to feel his fingers wrap around her wrist.

"Why don't you sleep here?"

She could practically feel his body tight against hers. Her body tensed. Despite her best efforts, heat stained her cheeks. "I don't think that's a good idea."

"No sex."

Unable to help herself, she glanced at his lap. No erection tented the sheet. He followed her gaze and grimaced. "Not like I'm able, right? It's not you, it's me. Trust me, my flesh is just a little on the weak side right now. If I was at full speed, watching you drink soup would have gotten me hard."

Genevieve stared at him, not quite sure how to respond. Was he trying to...reassure her?

"I'm screwing this up, right?" He rubbed his hand over his face and sighed in a gust of noise. "I'm not a suave guy, but normally I'm not this stupid. Look, I'm not going to lie, I find you really attractive. But I wouldn't pounce on you even if I could get it up. I'm not into force. Hell, you can even make me weak if you want, like I offered before."

He was so damn direct. For a girl who hated games and liars, it was a refreshing change. Genevieve raised her chin. "I'm not scared of you. It wouldn't take me long to fight you off if I didn't want you." The key word being *if*. Because if she was really confronted with a gorgeous, amorous Alex who wanted her, she didn't know if she was principled enough to refuse him. "I, um, just really like my couch. So...good night."

He watched her go with such disappointment, she was beyond tempted to run right back into his arms. What was up with this guy? Yes, part of it was that inexplicable physical chemistry. But the scary thing was that emotional conduit that had opened earlier between them.

They were thrown together in a cozy little situation here. She needed to be the responsible, levelheaded one, since he clearly wasn't into that role. His laid-back, flirtatious personality was damn attractive.

She tried to remind herself of that for the next four hours as she tossed and turned on the lumpy couch in her sunroom. The back room was colder than the main area of the cabin, partly because it lacked a fireplace, but mostly because the wall of floor-to-ceiling windows faced a winter wonderland.

Oh, and there was no naked hunk to curl up next to. That definitely made a difference in terms of warmth.

She heaved a rough sigh and tried to count the individual snowflakes as they fell down. She'd gotten up to about a hundred when a low moan interrupted her.

Without a second thought, she leapt out of bed and darted into the front room, certain Alex had hurt himself. When he was within her sights, she pulled up short. He wasn't in severe pain, but he would be if he kept thrashing around like that. The moans were spilling from his half-open mouth with increasing frequency, his brow furrowed. He was uttering words, but they were so low and disjointed she had no idea what he was saying.

Genevieve approached him cautiously, not wanting to scare him or jolt him too hard out of whatever nightmare he was caught in. She knelt next to him and grabbed his uninjured shoulder, giving him the slightest of shakes. "Alex. Wake up. You're okay."

His eyes popped open, but by their glassy appearance, Genevieve knew he didn't see her. "Jerry." His tone was low and filled with such naked pain, Genevieve's heart clenched a little. Who was Jerry?

She kept her tone firm and commanding. "No, it's Genevieve. You're dreaming."

He blinked a few times and awareness returned. "Genevieve?"

She knew she should remove her hand, but it felt good over the tensile strength of his shoulder. "Yes. You had a bad dream. Are you okay?"

Alex shook his head, as if to clear it. "Yes. I'm sorry. Did I wake you?"

No, 'cause I never slept, 'cause I was too busy thinking of your hot bod. "No. Don't worry about it."

"I haven't had that dream in a while."

Alex had some kind of effect on her verbal filter, because despite the fact that she knew it was none of her damn business, she couldn't help but ask, "Do you want to talk about it?"

He closed his eyes. "I'm all right."

She should have been relieved. Hadn't she just been telling herself that she needed to keep her distance from the oh-so-charming man? Without saying anything more, she moved as if to stand up.

"It's just that..."

Her butt hit the ground so fast it was like she was a toddler running for story time. She couldn't even begin to work up some good shame over her hypocrisy. "Yes?"

"I was shot last year while I was working a case. I think this stirred up that memory, that's all."

"Your leg, right?"

He cast her a startled glance and then gave her a halfhearted grin. "The sponge bath. Right. Yes."

Since he was being so chatty, she decided to go for broke. "Who's Jerry?"

Alex inhaled sharply. "I was talking, huh? Jerry's my partner. He died."

There was more to the story than that, but she didn't want to probe at what was obviously a very painful subject. "I'm sorry."

"It's not your fault."

"Will you be able to go back to sleep?"

He stared at the ceiling. "Sure."

She didn't need to view his aura to know he was lying. The waves of sadness and grief he was giving off would have been visible to anyone with a shred of empathy. Since those were emotions she was extremely familiar with, she couldn't leave him to stay awake all night. For one thing, it would undo her hard work, leave him vulnerable to becoming ill again.

Yeah, you're a regular Mother Teresa. "Do you want me to sleep with you?"

"There's no way I could ever say no to that question." His tone was dry. "Unless you're just doing it 'cause you pity me or something."

"Do we have to psychoanalyze it? Can't I just sleep here because it's the practical thing to do?"

His grin was a hell of a lot stronger than before. "Sure. I love practicality, though probably not to the level you do."

"Good. You're sleeping under the covers. I'll sleep on top."

She wished she had a shirt that would fit him. Hell, she wished she had full body armor to throw on him. Whatever kept him covered and out of temptation's reach.

"No, I'll sleep on top of the covers."

"If you argue, I'll go sleep on the couch."

He smiled. "Fine. You sleep on top of the sheet. Stay under the blanket?"

"Fine then. Do you need to use the bedpan?"

His face flushed. "I hate to have to do that."

"I've taken care of people when they've been sick. I don't mind."

"I do. I'm fine."

Grateful she was wearing her thickest, largest granny gown, she scooted in under the covers. Trying to keep his flesh from touching hers was an exercise in futility. He was so there, long and hard and male. Thankfully, he was no longer steeped in that awful sadness, but he threw off testosterone tempered by a caution and control that was more than exciting.

They lay on their backs, rigid, for a while. The firelight danced over the ceiling. With a low sigh, he tried to turn over onto his injured side and bit off a curse. Instead, he reached out his hand and groped for hers. "Can you come a little closer? Please?"

Genevieve could have refused but didn't bother, the plea in his tone her undoing. She scooted closer to his warmth until she was snuggled against his side. He wrapped his arm around her and tugged her even closer, so there was barely any room separating the two of them.

She'd almost rather he jumped her. Sex she could handle, but this cuddling was so sweet and gentle it made an ache open up in her chest.

Yeah, the idea of sex with him didn't alarm her at all. In fact, she figured it was close to inevitable, if they were sleeping together like this. She closed her eyes and laid her head on his chest, listening as his breathing evened out and deepened.

Chapter Six

Alex woke up with an armful of soft woman. In her sleep, with her defenses down, Genevieve had wiggled even closer until she lay sprawled over his uninjured side. Somehow, he must have kicked aside the sheet separating them, and her thick nightgown had ridden up to her waist. Her arm was wrapped around his chest, her leg thrown over his body so her thigh lay right over his hard cock.

He froze. Yes, he was hard beneath his boxers, his penis engorged in his usual morning erection, no doubt intensified by the female flesh cushioning it. He tipped his head back and fought the urge to cry in happiness. At the very least, he was back to normal below the waist.

Genevieve murmured and shifted, rubbing the plump flesh across the sensitive head. His tears of happiness turned into tears of frustration. He counted to ten very slowly, tightening his buttocks to keep from grinding up against her.

He hadn't been lying last night; his reasons for sleeping with Genevieve had been nonsexual. Selfish, but nonsexual. He had wanted to feel her against him, needed the connection of another human being. Maybe it had been an affirmation that he was alive.

What's more life affirming than sex?

No, Genevieve's trust was more important than sex. During

the hours he'd spent lying alone yesterday, he'd realized that his father's voice while he'd been crawling to safety may not have been a hallucination. What if he'd been guided to Genevieve? The only question was, to what purpose? How was he meant to help her?

Genevieve had been hurt, no question about it. He was good at mysteries. He'd uncover her secrets, and then he'd know how to help her. Something he had said or done must have resonated for her yesterday, since she'd lowered her guard enough to tease him and sleep in his bed. No way was she ready to trust him completely, but it was a start.

Maybe she can help you too.

He rejected that little taunting voice. He didn't need help. That dream last night had just been brought about because of the similarity of the two injuries, that was all. He'd gone through therapy, overcome his deepest depression about Jerry's death. Alex had moved on, had a new job. So what if he wasn't the same happy-go-lucky guy he'd been before last year? People changed. So what if his new job often felt like he was just a cop in name only? He was still a cop. He'd grown up in a police station, tagging along with his father. He'd been born to serve, and he'd die a cop, just like his old man.

No, the focus here was on Genevieve. She was the one who needed him.

She rubbed her thigh against him again and he bit off a curse. Could he help her without fucking her through the mattress? He didn't know. Alex didn't believe in casual sex. He'd personally never really had a one-night stand, had never really understood the appeal of making love to a stranger. Despite her tough talk, Alex had the feeling that Genevieve wasn't exactly the type who could have anonymous sex and move on, either.

At the same time, he was nobody's fool. There was some

weird connection between them that made him feel like he'd known her forever. He was wildly attracted to the woman. He understood that a lot of it was probably psychological, since she'd saved him, but that was mixed in with a healthy dose of old-fashioned physical lust. If the opportunity arose, and if she was consenting, he would probably have sex with her despite the short period of time they'd had together.

Since he couldn't fuck her and leave, that meant if they did have sex, he'd have to maybe...stay around? He glanced down at her face, her full cupid's-bow mouth open, close to his nipple. It would take him a while to get tired of looking at that face, if he ever did. She was special, no question about it, and it wasn't only because of her unexplainable power.

Of its own volition, his hand spread where it lay on the curve of her ass and he gently squeezed the flesh, luxuriating in the way it gave beneath his fingers.

His cock jerked, as if to get his attention. He released her ass and grabbed her thigh, intending to ease her leg off him. Instead, for a brief second, he held her there and thrust his hips the slightest bit, imagining the resilient flesh to be the slick recesses of her pussy.

Immediately he was ashamed of himself. He wasn't an animal, to molest a sleeping woman. With a bit more force than necessary, he removed her leg from him. As she murmured and blinked awake, he pressed his palm flat against his cock where it peeked above the waistband of his boxers and rearranged the comforter on top of his hips, bunching it to avoid any detection.

She stretched next to him, rather like a lazy cat. He wanted to pet her, but since he'd already done quite a bit of unnecessary petting, and his hands were currently busy trying to keep his cock under the radar, he didn't feel as if it was appropriate.

Genevieve turned her head and gave him a slow, lazy smile that warmed his heart. Yeah, he could definitely get used to waking up to that sight, as often as she'd let him.

He knew the exact instant when comprehension returned to her. Her face flushed and she scrambled away. If she thought they were in an inappropriate embrace now, he was thankful she hadn't woken up five minutes earlier. Her face would have caught fire.

"Morning." His voice was gravelly, despite the water she'd woken him to drink during the night.

"Good morning." After she had covered up her legs she turned to him. "How do you feel?"

"Better." His reply was automatic, but as he took stock of his body he realized that he did feel better. When he'd gotten shot last year, it had taken him almost two weeks to feel as great as he did today, just a few short days after he'd sustained a far more serious injury.

She left the room, and he did his best to think of as many unarousing thoughts as he could manage to cool his amorous body off. By the time he started reciting baseball stats for the Yankees, he knew he would be able to at least speak to her without embarrassing himself.

When she returned to the room, dressed in her faded jeans and a pink long-sleeved shirt, he had himself under control. Thank the good Lord, since she immediately tried to help him with his embarrassing morning rituals. "I can walk today, I think." Anything to get away from the bedpan.

"That's nice that you think that. You won't be doing it, though."

He groaned. "Please, Genevieve."

She eyed him critically. "Two more days before you're up and about. And if you complain anymore, I'll make it three."

"These are not the kind of orders I like to take in bed, *chica*."

A warm flush filled her face, but then she delighted him by retorting, "I don't see you taking any kind of orders in bed."

He grinned, a slow smile of intent. Ahh, yes, if she trusted him enough to flirt with him, he was a happy man. He'd never been much of a flirt, but he liked their banter, and sexual innuendos were tripping off his tongue around her. "You're right. I'm usually on top."

"Don't be crude." She didn't look insulted, though, just a very flushed armful. A militant look entered her eyes. "Bedpan, with me in the room or without. Your choice."

Since she wouldn't be budged, he gave in with a grumble and took care of his needs once she left the room.

When that chore was over, they enjoyed breakfast. Or rather, she enjoyed breakfast, and he choked down pasty gruel. "I'm vowing to you right now, when I get better, I'm cooking for you, and you're going to eat it. Everything I make is terrible, so we'll be even."

She didn't respond. She just crunched into her piece of toast, slathered with butter, and licked her shiny lips.

He made a woeful noise and she snickered. Genevieve probably had no idea he was reacting to her pretty lips instead of the toast.

As she cleaned up from breakfast, he tried to find a comfortable position, but each way he turned either made him more twitchy or hurt his shoulder.

"Stop squirming. You're going to hurt yourself."

"Men don't squirm. I'm itchy." He rubbed at his bandage.

"Don't touch that."

He dropped his hand to his lap. "Distract me then."

She blinked. "How?"

Strip naked. "What do you do for entertainment?"

"Entertainment?"

"Yeah. You know, that stuff that unpractical people do?"

"Impractical."

"Just a little, but I am a responsible guy."

"No. The word. It's not unpractical. It's impractical."

"Hey. You cook like the nuns at elementary school and you correct grammar like them too." Alex gave her a slow grin. "If you'd been my teacher though, I would have definitely paid more attention."

She fought it, but he noted with satisfaction the instant her smile got the best of her. "Give me a break."

"So what do you do?"

"There's always plenty to do on a small farm."

"But that's work. We're talking fun."

"I knit."

That surprised him. She was so pragmatic and no-nonsense, knitting seemed almost too soft. "That's cool. What do you make?"

"Blankets. Socks. I crochet a bit. Sell the stuff down at this tourist-trap store in Newbury."

He resisted the urge to smile. Of course Genevieve would make crafts practical. "My mom's a seamstress. She loves that stuff. You must have fun with that."

"It brings in some cash." Her tone was indifferent, as if she could take it or leave it.

"What else?"

She hesitated. "I read. Write. But mostly I spend a lot of time outside."

None of her activities included other people. It sounded so solitary. Alex was a social creature. Except for that dark time last year, he couldn't remember when he hadn't surrounded himself with a bunch of people. "That's it?"

"Movies. Do you like movies? I have a DVD player."

He wanted to weep with gratitude and a little bit of relief. Finally, a sign that Genevieve was a fairly normal young woman. "I love movies."

"Action, I'm guessing?"

"Sure."

Alex watched her walk out the back door and return with a portable DVD player and a stack of DVDs. She set up the player without speaking. When she moved to rise, he stayed her with a hand on her arm.

As soon as he touched her, electricity shot up his arm, and he knew it had nothing to do with magic. Just pure, old-fashioned chemistry. "Don't you want to watch with me?"

"It's the middle of the day."

He smiled at her slightly askance look. He figured she'd react the same way to a suggestion of making love during the day.

At first, that is.

"You can't watch a movie in the middle of the day? I mean, it's not like you can go outside and do anything." She was wavering, his instincts told him, so he pushed. "Come on. I'd love to watch with you."

She heaved a sigh and sat cross-legged next to him. He liked the position, since her jeans tightened around those round thighs. Mmm, that soft inner thigh which had been riding his... Oh crap.

Queen of England. Naked. On a snowdrift.

"Are you okay? You have a funny look on your face."

I'm trying to keep my dick calm, since there's only my boxers and a comforter between it and your face. "I'm fine. Which movies?"

She shot him a warning look, reaching for the stack of DVDs. "One movie. That's about all you'll be able to stand before your nap."

Alex gritted his teeth at the reminder of his invalid status. "Sounds good." Good for starters, at least. He settled into his pillows, certain he wouldn't be able to remember a single thing about the upcoming movie with Genevieve's delicate floral scent wafting under his nose.

Chapter Seven

"I'm bored with movies."

Genevieve rinsed the last dish from breakfast. They'd had fun watching four movies yesterday, breaking for meals and the chores she'd half-fabricated so he'd sleep. Normally she hated talking during movies, but the cheesy action flicks had lent to a teasing commentary running back and forth between them. After the second film, it had seemed easy to curl up next to his pallet. By the time the fourth movie rolled around, his arm had been around her shoulders. It had been a natural progression.

It was like some sort of spell was over the cabin. She could almost believe the real world didn't exist outside the snowed-in home. He wasn't really the police chief; she wasn't the town witch.

She hadn't even quibbled about sleeping in the same bed with him last night. As much as he might exchange sexual banter with her and touch her with easy familiarity, he was very careful to keep their touch platonic in bed. Until they fell asleep and their subconscious took over. Genevieve had found herself lying on top of Alex in the early hours of the morning, treating him like her very own mattress.

She shook herself out of that pleasant memory when he spoke. "What can we do today?"

Her lips quirked. The man was showing definite signs of

mending. As much as she knew he'd enjoyed their film marathon yesterday, such a virile guy was not well suited to lying around in bed. "Here's an idea...how 'bout you rest?"

"All I do is rest."

"Stop touching your bandage."

He grunted behind her. "How do you know I'm touching my bandage?"

She turned around as he dropped his hand away from his shoulder with a guilty look. "Lucky guess."

"Got any cards? Or board games?"

"A little of both."

"Excellent. Bring them."

"You're assuming a lot, that I can just drop everything to entertain you."

"Please? I'm going to die of boredom if you don't help me."

The man was just too hard to resist. She wavered under his pleading eyes. "A couple of rounds of cards. That's it." She brought a deck of cards from one of her cupboards to where he sat.

Without her assistance, he hauled himself up higher on the pillows. His face was alight with anticipation. Despite his easygoing attitude, Genevieve had a feeling Alex was probably about as competitive as she was, which made her happy. "How 'bout we make this a little more interesting?" he asked.

Ahh yes, maybe even more competitive. "How much you talking about?"

"Clothes?"

She laughed. "You lose right now, then."

Alex looked aggrieved. "It's not my fault I'm naked. Some chick cut all my clothes off and won't give me any more."

"Won't give you...I don't have any more, idiot. None that'll fit you at least."

"That's your story. Admit it, you just like to stare at my chest." He puffed out his aforementioned chest, and then winced.

She snorted in an effort to control the drool collecting in her mouth. "Yes, your manly, beat-up chest."

"Well, now that we've established we can't play strip poker 'cause you like to look at my nipples"—he raised a hand and spoke over her sputtering—"then I say we play for information."

She narrowed her eyes. "What kind of information?"

"For every game you win, you can ask me any question in the world. For every game I win, the same rules apply."

Genevieve hesitated. As attractive as the proposal sounded to learn a bit more about him, there were some areas she just wasn't at liberty to talk about. "What if there's something one of us doesn't want to answer?"

"Then you pay a forfeit." He grinned wickedly. "A kiss."

Well, hell, she'd forfeit right then and there. "In your dreams."

"Hopefully. What are you worried about, anyway? Just don't lose. Think about it. You can ask me anything you want, and I have to answer it."

"Fine. What game?"

"Lady's choice."

"Rummy." That was her game, and she would beat his figurative pants off.

Sure enough, she slapped her hand down in less than ten minutes and grinned. "That was easy."

"Show-off. Okay, what's your question?"

She paused. She had planned to ask him about his family, but her mouth opened and instead she heard: "Describe your ideal woman."

"We're getting personal? Nice. In looks or temperament?"

She wanted to squirm with embarrassment. She should laugh the question off, ask something else... "Both."

"In looks? Like you."

"If you're not going to be serious, we can play for peanuts or something."

"Why do you think I'm not serious?"

"You're just flirting with me like you've done since you woke up."

"And why do you think that is? I don't sleep around, and I don't have hundreds of girlfriends. I'm being dead honest. I think you're beautiful. The way you look is perfect—your body, your hair, your eyes. It's my ideal package."

"Okay, whatever."

"You don't believe me. Why?"

She gave him an exasperated look. "I don't think I'm ugly, but I'm hardly anyone's idea of an ideal beauty, that's why. I'm way too large for my height—"

"Ugh! This obsession with skinny is beyond my comprehension. There is nothing Latinos love more than a woman who looks like a woman. Hell, my mother is far larger than you are, and my father was madly in love with her. I don't think I have a single aunt or female cousin who is as tiny as the media wants women to be. And their men love them." He paused. "I should say their significant others love them. One of my cousins, Eva, she's a lesbian. Regardless, I love the way you look. When I'm with a woman, I want something soft to hold onto, and when I look at your hips, I know I can grab them, and

79

when I squeeze them as I push inside of you, the flesh is going to give beneath my touch—"

He stopped when she clamped her hand over his mouth. Her face was hot, and honestly, she wasn't sure if it was with pleasure or arousal. "Okay. I get it."

He mumbled beneath her hand, and she lifted it. "What?"

"Do you believe me now?"

"Yes." She shouldn't have asked him, though, not at all. She had trouble resisting him when she'd assumed his flirtation was all for show. Knowing that he really, honestly wanted her, that he loved the way her body looked? It was going to be very tough.

"As for temperament, I want someone gentle and sweet. Someone kindhearted and protective."

One who would probably never point a gun at him, she thought cattily.

"Someone who will take in an injured man and help him even though she might be frightened of him, simply because it's the right thing to do. Someone who might act sassy and brash but has the most gentle of touches." He looked at her with probing eyes.

She glanced away, suddenly shy. Genevieve cleared her throat and looked down at the cards she was idly shuffling. "Great. Good answers. Okay, next round?" She won the next hand in even shorter time and was a bit dismayed. God knew what information he would share this round. She decided to stick to something safe, her original question. "Tell me about your family."

Alex relaxed. "I was born and raised in Brooklyn 'til I was about twelve and my dad died. After that, we moved to Westchester so my mom could be near her family. My brother and her still live up in New York."

"I've never had a sibling. What was that like?"

"You'll never meet a more sober, stick-up-your-ass person than Lincoln. I swear he programs bathroom breaks into his PDA. He's the black sheep of our family. Defense attorney."

Genevieve hid a grin. "Disgusting."

"Tell me about it." His tone was rife with affection.

"Wait...Alejandro and Lincoln?"

He snorted. "My mother named me after her brother, who my dad despised. She told him he could name the second child. Since Linc came along right after my dad finally obtained his citizenship and he was so proud to be American...well, who's more American than our sixteenth president? I think Linc got down on his knees daily and thanked God he hadn't been named Abraham. For a Hispanic kid to be called Lincoln was bad enough in our neighborhood."

She gave a fleeting smile, but then sobered. "How did your dad die?"

A shadow crossed his face. "He was a cop too. Shot during an armed robbery at a gas station. The kicker was that he was off duty. He had just stopped by to pick up some milk when a crack addict walked in and pulled a gun on the cashier. He tried to overpower the guy, took a slug in the chest and died en route to the hospital." Alex swallowed. "I can still remember opening the door to the uniforms who showed up to tell us. My mom took one look at them and just grabbed me and my brother and started to sob. The fear of every cop's spouse, I guess."

She was silent for a second. "I'm sorry. That sucks."

"Yeah."

"He sounds like he was a good cop, though. Not all of them are."

He looked up sharply. "Sounds like you have a personal reason to say that."

She began to deal. "Nuh-uh. Not your turn to ask questions."

He must have been motivated, because he declared rummy. She waited, stomach knotted, for him to ask her why she disliked police. She'd have to forfeit, because she couldn't talk about that, wouldn't talk about it with anyone. Would his lips taste sweet or spicy? Would he use his tongue? Did he expect her to?

"Genevieve?"

"Huh?"

"Do you not want to answer?"

His tone was even, so she wasn't sure if he was happy about that prospect or not. "I'm sorry, can you repeat the question?"

"Tell me about your family and your childhood."

"That's two questions."

"You asked me how my dad died and about my family. We'll be even then."

Actually, that wasn't bad. She didn't know if she would be able to perform the forfeit without passing out from excitement, so she'd rather answer the easy ones. "I never knew my father. I grew up in this cabin with my mom."

"Was she like you? Gifted?"

"You mean weird? Yup. She hated to go into town. We went maybe once a month to Harrison when I was younger, not too often. She home-schooled me till I was about thirteen, then I put my foot down and insisted on going to a normal school." She smiled. "Mom was actually pretty decent about the whole thing. She'd drive me in her old Ford pickup every Monday and pick me up every Friday. I stayed with the daughter of one of her only friends." She peered at him. "Ron White?"

Alex frowned, and then put a face to the name. "The old grocer?"

"Yeah. He was so sweet, and a great male influence for me. I loved staying with them." As disloyal as it felt to her mother, that had been another of those *normal* times in her life that Genevieve hugged to her chest.

"After I graduated, I went to the University of West Virginia."

"Did you finish?"

She smiled, remembering her mother's pride when she had earned her major. "Yes. English major. I loved to read."

When she fell silent, he prompted her. "And then what? You came back to live here?"

"I spent a few years working at this newspaper. Then, yes, I came to live here. Mom—Mom was sick. She died two years ago."

"What did she die of?"

Me. "Cancer."

"I'm sorry, love." His voice was heavy with regret. They didn't speak for a little while. Alex took the cards from her and shuffled them in his hands. "Why did you stay after she died?"

Penance. Not that she could say it. "You've asked way more than two questions. Either deal, or let me go do some work."

He shut up and dealt another hand. This game went on for much longer, and while they played, Alex teased and bantered. By the time he won with a satisfied smirk, Genevieve was in a much better mood.

She tensed, though, certain he would continue the earlier line of questioning. Instead, he gave her a naughty grin. "So.

Who's your ideal man?"

She blushed and contemplated forfeiting. Not because she didn't want to answer the question, but because the answer was self-evident, and she really wanted to kiss him.

"Let me help you." He picked up her hand and played with her fingertips. Sensations tingled through them everywhere he touched. "We'll skip past personality because it goes without saying that he'd be someone smart, hilarious and attentive to your every need." He waggled his dark brows at her, and her lips quirked.

"Let's move on to looks." He brought her hand to his head, and she threaded her fingers through the coarse silk without any coaxing from him. "He'd be dark?"

Genevieve licked her lips. "I've always been partial to blonds."

"Hmm. There's hair dye." Still holding on to her hand, he brought it down his neck until it lay over his hard pec. "You'd want a bit of chest hair on him, I'm guessing."

God, he had the perfect amount of hair on his body, a smattering on his chest that arrowed down into his boxers. "I prefer men who wax."

He shuddered. "If that's what it takes." He drew her hand down farther to his belly. His hard, rippled, six-pack belly.

You've touched him here before. Stay cool.

Alex smirked. "You'll want someone strong?"

"Unnnh-huh." She swallowed. "I mean, I really love potbellies. Paunches."

"I'll start eating as soon as someone starts feeding me."

"I love your body," she said in a rush, her honesty taking over.

His hand stilled over hers. He grinned, a full-fledged, ear-to-ear kind of thing. "I'm glad," he said simply.

"Is it hypocritical that I don't have a hard body, but I like that you do?"

His thumb rubbed the back of her hand. "I work out because I enjoy it, and I need to stay fit for my job. I'm thrilled you like the results of that work, but like I told you, I love the way you look right now. So, no."

That little stroking thumb was driving her crazy, to say nothing of the muscles moving beneath her palm. She could slide her hand right below the cover and the sheets, encircle his penis...

She glanced down, and her eyes widened at the tent in the blanket. He followed her gaze and grimaced. "I'm sorry."

"I thought you couldn't..."

"I can. I probably can't do a lot with it right now, but I can at least...get it up." His tone was wry.

Genevieve was suddenly short of breath. She'd never been quite so attracted to someone. Though she knew what she was doing wasn't very smart, she looked up and met his gaze. "I think I should have to pay a forfeit."

His eyes flared. "Yeah?"

"Well I didn't exactly answer your question, you kind of guided me."

He leaned a bit closer, and she realized she'd swayed closer as well. "I'd say you're right..."

His hand slipped behind the nape of her neck and drew her down.

Man, the guy could kiss. He made no allowances for his invalid status, he just angled her head and dived right in. It didn't take her long to respond to his enthusiasm. She was the first one to flick her tongue out against his lips. He grunted and tangled his against hers, then flicked it into her mouth, over and over. When she became more aggressive, nipping at his lower lip and drawing it into her mouth to suckle it, he groaned and sank his other hand into her hair.

Passion overtook her brain. She no longer cared about who he was or where he was from. All that mattered was that he was a man, she was a woman, and they wanted each other very badly. Everything else could work itself out later.

His palm slid down her throat, continuing until he completely covered her breast. He didn't even have to do anything else; the mere touch of his hand caused her nipple to harden. Her fingers clenched on his belly, kneading the hard flesh. He squeezed her breast in reaction.

His next sound was more shocked as her hand slid lower, taking the covers with it, until her palm rested over his groin. His cock was so hard, the fat tip had punched out past the elastic waistband of the boxers.

He tore his mouth away from hers. Both of them were breathing heavy. They stared at each other for a moment, connected physically through the intimate touch on her breast and his cock. The cotton separating their flesh could just as well been nonexistent.

God it felt so good, the passion and excitement rolling inside of her. No guilt or worries, though they would probably come later.

He raised his other hand to her, but she caught the flinch as his injury pulled. Genevieve linked her fingers through his and brought it down to his side. "Stop moving."

His smile was a baring of teeth. "I told you I don't take orders in bed well."

The spurt of power surprised her. "You don't have any choice right now, though, do you? Stay still."

When he froze, she questioned her method. What exactly did she hope to accomplish here?

"Kiss me again," he murmured.

Well, that she could do. She leaned in, savoring every second of the moment.

This kiss was slower, a natural progression of rising lust. It seemed right to keep her hand over his cock, to try to get rid of the barrier. He raised his hips slightly when she slid his boxers out of the way and caught the heavy weight of his erection in her hand. He gasped as if she'd goosed him with an electrical current.

She drew away and looked down. The tip of his penis was already wet, the dark skin stretched and tight. A stab of uncertainty hit her. "Tell me if I do something wrong. I haven't done this in a while."

"Are you kidding me? You touching me...it's like a dream. Besides, it's been a long time for me too," he admitted.

"I wouldn't think you'd have a problem finding a lover."

"I've been busy. I'm particular." His eyes literally rolled back when she grasped his cock. "God, that feels good."

"You're not busy now."

"No."

Genevieve tightened her hand around his penis, stroking up and using the bead of pre-come at the tip to ease her way. It was unnerving how he watched her with those black eyes. There was pleasure there, but she detected a hint of dissatisfaction. "What's wrong?"

"Nothing. It's just that I want to touch you too."

Her body yearned for him. "Next time."

"Will there be a next time?"

What was the point in being demure? His breath hissed out

as her hand tightened on him. "Yes."

When he became greedy, though, and started to arch his hips into her touch, she stopped and placed her other hand on his stomach. "No moving or you'll hurt yourself."

He stilled instantly.

Ooooh. This is fun.

Genevieve lost herself in touching his body, taking control of his pleasure. His quiet gasps and the slight slap of his flesh in hers filled the room. There was an erotic charge in handling his race to orgasm as he lay there helpless.

He wrapped his other hand around hers, tightening her fingers far more than she would have on her own. "Harder. Faster now."

She gave special attention to that little area under the mushroomed head, and he muttered curse words in rising pleasure. "Fuck, I'm going to come."

Her thighs clenched in excitement. She wanted to see him come, wanted to watch him reach completion. His big golden body was stretched taut. She sped her strokes until his hips arched and he gave a shout. Streams of semen shot out of his cock to land on his rippled abs. She stared at the display. Something that had always seemed rather messy and unpleasant looked...wonderful.

Mine.

Genevieve blinked, a bit startled at that dark, possessive whisper in her mind. Yes. That semen didn't belong on him, it belonged on her, in her. He was hers, completely.

And she was his. Completely.

Her body shook, partly with unappeased desire, but mostly with fright. No, she belonged to no man.

Liar.

She couldn't be in a relationship.

Too bad.

Stop it!

"Genevieve?"

She blinked, brought his worried face into focus. What had she been thinking?

She hadn't. Like a man, she'd been thinking with her libido. "You look tired. We shouldn't have done this."

"If I was well...if we'd met normally...would you want to?"

"What, have sex?"

"Yes."

Hell, yes. "Maybe."

His black eyes burned. "I'm going to be well. Very soon."

Genevieve shivered at the promise in his tone. "It would just be sex though. Nothing else." She wasn't at liberty to promise anything else.

"We'll see."

"You shouldn't overdo anymore now."

Alex gave a short laugh. "No kidding. Tell that to Mr. Happy."

At that prompt, she glanced down at his erection, which, sure enough, poked up against the sheets, as if it hadn't just been thoroughly satisfied. Well she couldn't blame him. She knew with certainty she wouldn't be sated until she had him inside of her. Many, many times.

And that scared the pants off her.

"Let's take it a bit slower, okay?" He spoke softly, as if he were dealing with a timid animal. "Why don't you get me a towel, and we can play something else? We can talk a bit more, get to know each other. How's that?"

She considered it. Okay, yes. This she could handle. After all, it wasn't like she could run away from him. Where would she go?

Despite her bone-deep certainty that this man would change her life, could easily make her forget her vow, make her forget everything important, she didn't want to leave him. She wanted to laugh and joke and talk with him, and when he was able, she fully intended to have sex with him.

Call her stupid. She couldn't help herself. Genevieve stood. "Sounds good. Let me get a towel. Be right back."

When she reached the door, he called out behind her. "You're an arsonist on the run. That's why you hate cops."

Her lips twitched, a glimmer of her normal sassiness returning as she tossed her hair. "Soot makes me sneeze. Guess again."

Chapter Eight

It would be hell if he survived a gunshot wound, infection, dehydration and exhaustion only to die of sexual frustration.

Alex shot a quick glance at Genevieve across the chessboard they were sharing. Her eyes were cast down, her lashes long crescents resting against her cheeks. She nibbled at her lower lip and he almost groaned. Damn it, he loved it when she did that.

He sighed and looked down at the chessboard. After their run of cards had ended so spectacularly two days ago, they'd tacitly decided to turn to other modes of enjoyment. Yesterday had been Scrabble; chess today. Alex had been unnerved by the emotions that had flashed across Genevieve's face after their passionate session together. He didn't want to spook her, cause her to run because she was scared of the heat that exploded between them. The emotions too. He couldn't believe these strong feelings were one-sided. They had to be returned, right? God, he hoped so.

So he'd decided to be gallant if it killed him. No more sex until a) he was healed enough to give her the unbridled pleasure she deserved and b) he was well enough to snuggle off any of her fears after the fact.

They still slept together at night, and Alex hated it and loved it in equal measure. Having her body pressed against him without sinking inside of her was an exercise in torture, but she smelled so sweet and she became incredibly soft and cuddly after she fell asleep.

"Queen me."

He refocused on the game and gave a silent groan to see her pawn had made its journey. He was proud to say he'd won the first couple of games they'd played. Then he'd started noticing things, like the way her breasts peeked out over the neckline of her shirt, or how she licked her lips while thinking, and he'd started a losing streak that hadn't quit.

You are not controlled by your cock.

Great. Now someone just needed to tell Mr. Hopeful that. Alex figured the guy was getting back at him for making some very unpopular decisions about their sex life.

"Checkmate."

He looked down, unsurprised to see the truth in that. "Congratulations. Again."

"Don't worry. I'm pretty good. You'll get better."

He'd gone to state championships back in high school. He sighed. "Okay, what's your question?" The question-and-answer thing they'd continued, though Alex had toned down the sexual nature of his questions to go along with their mutual agreement to wait. He'd learned quite a bit about her and her life, probably more than she even realized she'd told him.

She'd painted a picture of a lonely little girl who'd always been different, who lived alone with her beloved mother isolated in the woods, who had craved normalcy and embraced it when she'd left for school and work. She'd kept her gift hidden from everyone, pretended to be just like everyone else, and loved life, thriving in the middle of a busy city.

Until she hit twenty-three. Since she was twenty-six now,

Alex figured that had been the age when something had happened. It was like her life had ended at that point. She wouldn't speak of anything after it, nor would she speak of the future. She made monthly trips to Newbury for provisions, made enough to live on by selling her crafts to a gift shop, but it didn't seem as though she had any burning passion for that job. She seemed to view it as just a way to make a few bucks and survive. When he'd asked what she wanted to be when she grew up, instead of answering him, she'd pressed a soft kiss against his lips in forfeit. Her eyes had been so heavy with sadness, he couldn't bring himself to badger.

He knew she'd returned to take care of her mother, but why she had stayed after her death was a mystery. Likewise, despite his half-teasing questions, he still didn't know why she didn't trust cops.

He watched her study him. So far he'd answered each of her questions honestly, no matter how painful. He'd spilled everything about his father's death, his first girlfriend, the first time his mother had dated another man, and the list went on and on. Alex hoped his openness would encourage her, would show her how much he trusted her on faith alone. Otherwise, he was really bleeding his veins out here for her.

He braced himself for another doozy, and he received it. "Why did you move down here?"

Alex froze, seriously contemplating a forfeit for the first time.

"If you don't want to talk about it, I can ask another question."

Her expression was so soft and open, he couldn't fabricate or not talk about it. Besides, his department-appointed therapist had urged him to discuss the experience with people. He didn't know how much he believed in that psychology shit, but if he wanted Genevieve to open up to him, he couldn't be a pussy about it himself.

"I told you my partner died last year. I was narcotics, and we were conducting some surveillance on this mid-level dealer. We followed him to an abandoned warehouse. I called in backup as soon as we realized it was the drug deal we were waiting for, and then we took up place to watch and wait."

He paused, remembering the exact instant Tom Leonie's head had jerked up, the second the dealer had realized someone else was in that abandoned building. "To this day, I don't know what noise Jerry made, how they knew where he was. I could see him jerking and spinning, and in a minute, I knew he was dead. No way he could have survived that many shots.

"I took one slug in the thigh when I returned fire, not that it helped much. I couldn't draw my weapon fast enough to save Jerry." Alex coughed to clear the rough sound of his voice. "Firing after the fact didn't help anything. Backup showed up right after I got hit. Great for me, but no good for him."

Her voice wasn't horrified, but reasonable. "How many guys were you up against?"

"Four. One of them pulled the trigger on Jerry. All of them opened fire on me once I started shooting."

"Let me guess. You think you could have taken all of them out before they shot your partner?"

"How'd you know? It sounds crazy when you say it like that."

"I know a little something about guilt." Her tone was very dry.

"That's what the shrink told me. Survivor's guilt, she called it. I don't know. In reality, I know I couldn't have done anything, it was such a split-second thing. I can't help but feel like if I'd just responded a little faster... I'd known the guy since the academy. Had dinner with his family. I should've done something more. Instead, all I could do was wait. Sit there with his body no more than twenty feet away till backup showed up."

"I think you did the right thing." Genevieve surprised him by leaning forward and giving him an awkward hug. "I'm glad you're alive."

His heart expanded. She was so prickly, he relished this, her first overt expression of tenderness. He pulled her close until she cuddled against his chest. She was surprisingly accommodating.

"Anyway, after that, I had a tough time returning to work. To see Jerome's desk and the gym and even the coffee shop without him there, I was a mess. My brother heard about this job from his girlfriend's brother and, well, here I am."

"You didn't consider leaving police work? Something like that would make me seriously reconsider even staying in the same field."

"Are you kidding me? I'm third generation. My grandfather was the first Hispanic man on his force. I can't just stop being a police officer."

"That's not the only reason you're a cop, though, right?"

"No. Of course not. It's about serving, protecting. It's incredibly fulfilling."

"Is it still as fulfilling down here?"

Alex paused. It wasn't the same thing. He wasn't putting away the scum of the earth or keeping the public safe from anything more severe than jaywalkers. His job wasn't about fulfillment in Harrison. It was just...a job. But he was a cop. That was the important thing. Honestly, if he lost that title, he wasn't sure what he was.

Since he didn't want to contemplate it too severely, he tried to inject more enthusiasm into his voice than he felt. "Sure. Doesn't matter how big a town is. Everyone needs law and order."

Her smile was the softest he'd ever seen it. "I can tell you really believe in the system. That's great."

Alex raised a brow. "Why do I get the feeling you're patronizing me?"

"I'm not."

"I'm not naïve. There are shades of grey everywhere, I get that. But, yeah, for the most part, there's a right and a wrong way to go about things."

She was silent, but she didn't move from his arms. "Yeah. So you like living there?"

Alex tried to choose his words carefully, since he knew, for some reason, it mattered to Genevieve. "I like the pace. I like the size of the town, that I know who most people are, and they know me. The scenery's nice too. My apartment's decent. But it's not in my blood or anything, the way this place might be in yours."

"This place isn't in my blood."

So why do you stay? He didn't want to get into a fight though, not when she was curled so soft and sweet against him. He rubbed his chin against the top of her head. The strands got stuck in his beard. "Sorry."

She drew away, untangling them. "You need to shave."

Time for a lighter tone. "That would be wonderful. Got a razor?"

"Oh. Um. Sure. Hang on."

She escaped to the bathroom where she popped a new razor cartridge into her shaver and grabbed the other supplies he would need. Her hands were shaking, she was surprised to notice. His tale of woe had affected her more than she'd thought.

Damn it, she didn't want to see him hurt. Every hour that she spent with him, she fell a little bit more in...

Lust. That was all it was. Pure lust. "Just bang him and get it over with," she muttered to herself. Hell, why not? They both knew where this was headed.

She was still giving herself a pep talk when she returned to the room. She set down the towels, the bowl of hot water she'd drawn from the bathroom sink and the shaving supplies. "I brought you a mirror. Do you want me to hold it?"

He ran his hand over his jaw. "Actually, do you mind doing the shaving? I'm afraid to allow myself near my own throat with a razor. My hand's still shaky."

"You trust me with a blade to your throat?"

"I think I've established that I trust you with my life in every way," he said simply. She felt equally humbled and envious. How nice to be that certain of anything.

She cleared her throat. "Sure. You're going to smell like pomegranates. Hope that's okay." She held up the pink can of shaving foam she used.

He eyed the can warily. "Since I didn't know pomegranates even had a scent, I guess that will have to do. I don't mind if you don't."

Like she cared what his jaw smelled like. Unwilling to damage his trust, she took her time shaving him, leaving not a single nick on his rough skin. When she patted away the remaining foam, he smiled, revealing a heretofore unnoticed dimple in his cheek, and she caught her breath. She'd been wholly unsuccessful in resisting the charm of her scruffy, manly houseguest. But with his beard gone, Alex was simply beautiful, his features picture perfect. Had he showed up on her door looking like this, she probably would have dropped her panties on the spot.

Yeah, 'cause you're playing so hard to get.

"How do I look?"

"Great." Her throat was hoarse, so she tried again. "Really good."

"Thanks. I feel so much better. You know what else would help?"

Alex tucked a strand of her hair behind her ear in a blatantly possessive move. She'd gotten so used to his touch over the past couple of days, it no longer shocked her, though a thrill coursed through her limbs when he drew one finger down her cheek. The calluses rasped against her skin, and he captured her chin in his fingers. He held her trapped there, looking into her eyes.

And just that easily, the world was reduced to the two of them. While they were bantering and chatting, she'd try to convince herself that their physical chemistry was all a part of her imagination, but a touch, a look, and she was ready to melt again. "What would help?"

Alex tugged her closer, his breath fanning over her lips. Her nipples tightened, a response she was well accustomed to by now. "A bath. I would love a bath."

She cleared her throat and escaped his grasp. "That's tough." Her voice was rough, and she cleared her throat again. "I don't have a bathtub."

Alex raised his eyebrows. "I don't think I've ever met a woman without a bathtub."

"I have a perfectly fine shower," she said defensively.

"Yeah, but"—Alex shook his head, a bemused expression

on his face—"wouldn't you love to lounge in a bath of hot water every now and again? Most women I've known would rather die than be separated from their bath salts."

Oh, yeah, to linger in a bath of steaming hot water filled with sweet-smelling salts while Alex massaged foaming shampoo through the strands of her hair. Genevieve caught the whimper of longing before it rose from her throat. No, she was no different from most women. But her mother had been a no-nonsense woman who never encouraged the slightest bit of hedonistic behavior, and since her death Genevieve hadn't seen the point in installing a bathtub just for herself.

But oh, how she wished she had, for the pleasure of imagining Alex in it. To feel like a normal woman with a normal life.

She shook her head to disguise her longing. "That's pretty silly," she said briskly, gathering the shaving supplies up. "There are far more important things to die for than bath salts."

Alex's gaze sharpened. "Maybe you can tell me some of those things." He held up a hand. "In the meantime, shower?"

"One more day..."

"Genevieve, please. I'm feeling pretty grungy. I want to get clean. And I know I can make it. I can't lie here forever."

Genevieve's first instinct was to deny his claim, but then she studied him closely. His color was up, and he sat a lot easier now than he had at first. Part of his motivation was no doubt the desire to get away from the dreaded bedpan and her assistance with things like brushing his teeth, but he probably could make it on his own.

She felt equal amounts of satisfaction and sadness. The quicker he healed, the faster he would walk out of her life. He was fun and funny, and he had slipped right under her guard. "Okay, you win. Let's give it a try. Here, let me take off your bandage first."

She peeled it off him, pleased to see the wound's edges coming together nicely. The various scratches and bruises were almost nonexistent now, the bump on his head slightly visible. If she didn't know better, she would have sworn he'd been convalescing for a few weeks.

"What are you thinking?"

"That I'm pretty freakin' awesome."

He laughed and tested his arm's health with a slight rotation. "I'll second that. Now, scoot, I'm going to see if your awesomeness extends to my being able to walk."

With a minimum of assistance, he pushed his body off the bed and stood. When he was upright, his chest and legs did all sorts of muscular things that didn't happen prone. "I need to find you some clothes."

"It's so warm in here, I'd think you could walk around naked in the dead of winter and not feel a thing."

Nice thought. "My mom made sure the cabin was well-insulated."

He staggered a bit before he straightened and raised a hand to keep Genevieve from helping. The determined expression on his face told her he wanted to try to do this on his own. "I'm okay. Just caught me by surprise. Point me to this shower of yours."

He walked stiffly and she was sure it wasn't as easy as he tried to pretend. She led him to the back door and couldn't resist laying a hand upon his arm when he entered. He didn't protest the support since he was too busy looking around. "A sunroom? Was this added on to the structure? The front looks older."

She nodded and looked around the large room with its one

wall of glass and comfortable chairs and furnishings facing the light. "Right before I was born. The bathroom too." She gestured to the wooden door to the right and smiled. "Mom said she didn't want her baby growing up with an outhouse."

Alex raised an eyebrow. "I'm sure that's a sentiment most parents share. This room's really pretty. If I were you, I'd live out here."

Genevieve shrugged. "Sometimes I do." She led him to the bathroom and started the shower. When she turned around, he was leaning against the vanity for support. His boxers were at his feet and she was treated to one hell of a full frontal.

Her face flushed, and he looked amused. "Sorry. You've been touching me for days. I didn't think it was that big of a deal."

He'd been wearing something all this time though, whether it was boxers or a sheet. Plus, he'd been lying down. A bolt of lust arrowed through her. Genevieve had to fight to keep her eyes from skimming over his rangy legs, taut abs, long, thick...

"Get in the shower." She ignored his chuckle. Everything reminded her of sex all of a sudden, the showerhead, the mirror above the vanity, his big fingers as he grasped the shower wall for support. As he turned, she received the best present she'd ever gotten—her first look at the world's finest ass. Hard and carved out of muscle, they were two perfect globes of sexy, droplets of water from the shower dripping down to crest over the brown skin.

"Genevieve?"

"Hunh?"

His cheeks flexed, and the spell was broken. She looked up to find him grinning at her over his shoulder. "You want to touch?"

No, she wanted to bite. Nom, nom. "I don't know what

you're talking about. Here, let me adjust that nozzle spray for you." Without getting into the tiny cubicle, she stretched up so the water slicked over his head instead of his abdomen. Some water ran down her arm.

He made a low utterance of pleasure as the water cascaded over his hair, plastering the short strands to his skull. Genevieve tried to shake off her spell and leave, but he caught her gaze. "Can you help me soap up?"

Argh. Was he trying to come up with ways to drive her mad? However, the suggestion made sense. What if he fell? What if his marvelous ass got just a wittle bit bruised? No, let his ass remain in her hands. "Sure." She grabbed the bar with such enthusiasm it almost slipped through her fingers.

"Do you want to take your clothes off and come inside so they don't get wet?" His tone was so innocent, had she not become accustomed to the naughty sparkle in his eyes over the past couple of days, she might have been fooled.

"I'll manage." Genevieve set the soap on the vanity, rolled up the sleeves of her shirt and picked up her shampoo bottle. "Let me do your hair first." Safer.

Or so she thought. The coarse strands were practically begging for her to linger, though she kept her motions brisk while she washed and rinsed his hair.

Once that was done, she worked the soap into a rich lather and started at his shoulders as he braced himself on the shower wall. Had she not been touching him, she would have missed the fine tremors of strain running through his body. Not for the first time, she was impressed by his strength of will.

Just as she had seen his body before, she had certainly touched it as well, but this time felt different. Perhaps it was the slickness of his flesh beneath her palms, or the steam the shower generated, but by the time she had reached his ass, her touch had shifted from caring nurse to exploring lover.

When she knelt outside the small shower stall to wash the backs of his knees, her panties were already well on their way to soaked, her heartbeat accelerated. The water that splashed onto her didn't matter; she welcomed it as a reminder to keep her head in reality. She finished and took a deep breath, trying to speak past the need in her throat. "Turn around."

He turned, took one look at her kneeling at his feet and leaned back against the tiled wall. "Get up. Please."

Her inner temptress emerged to play. Who knew she had this slut living inside of her? Sure, she'd always liked sex, but she thought she'd repressed that side of her over the past few years, that she was satisfied with her dirty books and battery-operated boyfriends. Apparently not. "I haven't done this side yet. You were the one who wanted to be clean."

His jaw clenched, and Genevieve acknowledged that it was Alex who brought about this change in her personality. She'd never quite been the focus of so much male want before—it was a heady feeling.

You're the only woman here. Of course he's latched on to you. Genevieve ignored the cynical whisper. So what if this was an extraordinary reaction brought about by extraordinary circumstances? They were both consenting adults.

She finished washing the muscles of his thighs. His cock had hardened to full readiness, curving upward from a dark nest of curls. She grasped it with slick hands and soaped it up, gratified at the near whimper that emerged from his lips.

Genevieve lifted his cock slightly to wash his balls, and he shifted to accommodate her. "God yes."

Not even pretending to wash him anymore, she gently rolled his balls in her palm.

"Just like that...squeeze. Yes. Christ, Genevieve."

She released her hold to encircle his penis the way he had taught her. He grabbed hold of her hand before she could stroke him more than twice. "No. The next time I come, it's going to be inside of you."

She looked up at him, her body humming. "Are you well enough?" Because if he wasn't, then she was going to have to jack him off. That's how desperate she was to have her hands on him.

His expression was a flattering mix of elation and relief. "Hell yes. Come on."

She laughed as he tried to leave the shower. "Since you're in here, let me wash the rest of you." Without bothering to tease either of them, she soaped up his upper torso, careful to avoid getting too much soap near his injuries. Unable to resist, she leaned in for a quick lick of his small brown nipple, uncaring that the water splashed on her hair. He hissed.

She turned off the water and handed him a towel, not trusting herself to touch him. He dried himself off with rough motions and then wrapped the towel around his waist.

"Sit on the toilet seat and let me wrap up your shoulder again."

Once she was done wrapping a fresh covering, she dug under her cabinet to remove a blue box. When she looked at Alex, his expression was chagrined. "You know, I never even thought about protection."

The unopened box of condoms had been taunting her for the past few days in the back of her mind. "I'm on the pill, too, but you know."

"I thought it had been a while for you." His tone said it all. Why did she need either of those things if she was way up here in the middle of nowhere and had no intention of having sex?

"It has." She hesitated, and decided to be truthful. "I'm not stupid—I'm a woman living by myself. The birth control is my way of defending myself in case...anything happens. As for the condoms, I guess if someone's bent on forcing me, I can't do much about making them wear one. But it makes me feel safer."

His body had gone rigid while she spoke, his eyes blazing. "I can't believe you have to worry about that."

"Hey, I don't worry over it, but I'm a realist." Damn, she'd gone and killed the mood. She had the feeling that despite his tough job, Alex was a bit of an idealist. They'd both been knocked around, but he still seemed to believe the best of people.

He stood, his legs still wobbly enough that she had to brace him. He kissed the top of her head. "There's no force here."

"No. None at all."

"Grab the box."

"The box?" She'd been planning on one or two. Her lower body practically danced a jig in delight.

His slow smile was sex on a stick. "I'm optimistic."

When they emerged from the bathroom he stopped her before she could lead them to the front room. Genevieve followed his gaze to the overstuffed couch. "Here."

"There's a bed..."

"No. I want to see you framed by the snow." Uncaring of matters of modesty, he flung his towel aside and walked away to settle on the sofa. He sat down with a sigh. "I'm afraid you're going to have to be on top. I'll make it up to you later, I swear."

Like that would be a hardship. The way she was feeling right now, he just needed to sit there, and she'd be happy. She touched the bottom of her shirt. Without bothering to think about it too hard for fear she would lose her nerve, Genevieve whipped the cotton over her head and dropped it on the floor next to her. She unbuttoned her jeans and hesitated, those pesky nerves starting to whimper in distress. Though the snow made the day dreary, plenty of light lit the room. She'd always been a bit shy about her body.

Alex didn't seem to notice her hesitation, his eyes wide and fixed on her breasts in the heavy-duty utilitarian bra. She wished for the satin and lace she used to wear, but she'd gotten rid of all of those luxuries when she'd come back home. Her version of a hair shirt, so to speak. She had plenty of those.

When Alex reached out a shaking hand, she pushed the dark thoughts out of her head. "Are you feeling okay? You don't look too steady."

He gave a short laugh. "I'm shaking with lust, not illness. Get over here."

She stood in front of him. He scraped his nail over one of her nipples. Immediately, it and its companion responded, the nipples making obvious points against the bra. He grinned. "They like me."

"Surprise," she said dryly, and he laughed, then sobered.

"Are you okay with this?"

She hadn't been, but the way he looked at her breasts with such clear need had calmed her unease a bit. He wasn't eyeing her belly pooch or other imperfections with disgust.

All the same, everything had moved at such warp speed, she didn't know if she could handle being naked with him just yet.

Misunderstanding her hesitation, Alex removed his hand, his face wiped clean of expression. "I'm not rushing you. Put your clothes back on."

Her body was ready to howl in sadness at that idea. "It's

fine." Refusing to think about it anymore, she pushed her jeans over her hips and let them fall to the floor. Genevieve kicked them to the side.

His eyes were so big, Genevieve could see the whites all around his pupils. She could feel the touch of his gaze everywhere, up and down her legs, between her thighs, on her belly, her breasts. When he finally met her gaze, he spoke. "I adore your body. I worship it. I want to sink into it and never come up for air. Can you turn around and bend over for me?"

Whatever doubts she had vanished. She gave him a wicked grin. "Only if you're good."

"I can be as good as you want me to be. Why don't you take off that bra? It looks very uncomfortable."

Driven to please both of them, she obeyed. When she slipped her bra down her arms he licked his full lips in appreciation. As her panties hit the floor, his gaze traveled south. "You're so pretty. Come here."

She ripped open the box she'd tossed on the side table. Withdrawing a foil packet, she walked toward him, growing more confident with every step she took, despite the various jiggling she knew was going on. When she was within his arm's reach, he eased her forward with his hands on her hips. "I think these breasts were made for me. Look at these pretty nipples. They're so long."

She looked down. When erect, her nipples were rather long. It had always been a bit of an embarrassment. "Can't help it."

"I don't want you to. I love them. Are they sensitive? Do you like it when I do this?" He scraped his pinky nail against the tip.

Nice, but she needed more and arched toward him. He took his cue beautifully and captured her nipple between his thumb and forefinger, pinching until Genevieve gave a low, long moan of acceptance to spur him on.

"Will you like my mouth more?" He plumped her flesh higher and bent to draw the hard tip into his mouth. She panted as he sucked and laved it with his tongue, and gasped when he bit down gently.

"Alex, I really don't need any more foreplay."

He lifted his head and studied the nipples flushed red, hardened to tight little points. "God, angel, you're so sensitive. I could play with these forever." His forefinger nudged one nipple, and his eyes darkened as it instantly hardened and lengthened some more.

She straddled his lap so they were face to face. Though she knew no one was in her backyard, she felt mildly exposed from behind thanks to the glass wall the couch faced. However, it was worth it for the erotic thrill she knew he got from seeing her, as he had put it, framed by snow. He surveyed her briefly and then buried his face in her neck, biting and sucking the flesh while his hand quested down her body. She could feel every callus on his palm as he rubbed circles into the softly rounded flesh of her stomach.

He stroked lower until his fingers rested on the top of the triangle of curls that shielded her. He nibbled on her ear and whispered, "Can I shave you one day?"

Genevieve shuddered. "Would I like it?"

"I'd make sure you loved it."

Not only was she considering it, Genevieve was ready to go grab the razor. If the idea excited Alex as much as it seemed to, she figured she would probably love it too.

He didn't wait for her response, but dipped his fingers down to part her folds and slide a finger down her slit. She was creamier in just a few minutes with him than she had ever been on her own. "Mmmm, yeah, you're sweet."

The depth of her arousal would have embarrassed her had

she not been feeling so desperate. Her body made a squelching sound as he drove a finger inside her. His shudder echoed hers when he added another finger, thrusting deep with strong, smooth strokes. She gave a startled moan when he withdrew his hand and lifted her leg. "I'm not feeling too sure of my abilities to keep myself sitting and get inside you without embarrassing myself. Let me lie down."

They readjusted until he was lying on his back, one foot flat on the floor. His penis rose thick and long, the head almost bouncing off his bellybutton. He noted the direction of her gaze and rubbed her hip. "Don't be scared."

"I'm not," she assured him. She wasn't lying. With him under her, her body completely exposed to him, there was no wariness or distrust. Everything had been building toward this minute. She looked him straight in the eye and picked up the condom she'd tossed on the couch. "I want you inside of me."

"Let me put that on. I won't last two seconds if you get your hands on me again."

She was disappointed, since she'd wanted to smooth the latex down over him, but she consoled herself with the fact that he could probably do it faster. Sure enough, he was dressed to play in no time. When he reached down to part her folds and lodge the tip of his cock against her opening, she stopped him by grasping his penis in her fist. "You lie back. Let me handle this."

He opened his mouth to argue, but she shut him up with the expedient method of sinking down on him just an inch or two. He swallowed and tried again. "I'm calling the shots next time."

She snorted. "You haven't seen me calling the shots. Now hush." She was so wet, she didn't want to tease either of them. She hadn't been lying, she didn't need any more foreplay. Their dancing around each other for the past few days of constant contact had been foreplay enough.

She was ready, but it had been almost four years since her last lover. The bulbous head powered through her tight flesh, and before she could blink, she had seated him halfway inside her. She gave a strangled yelp at the sudden uncomfortable sensation. He froze and his eyes flared before they went vague with exquisite pleasure.

He held still within her body, both of them shuddering as her muscles adjusted to accept the hardness inside of her. After a few minutes, the uncomfortable fullness receded enough for her to focus on how good the intruder felt. She gave a tentative wiggle of her hips. She liked the resulting feeling so much she arched her hips and gasped as he sank inside another inch.

The small movements spurred him to action. He grasped her hips despite her directive to lie there. She couldn't really scold him when he was making her feel so damn good. In a few more thrusts, she was accepting his large cock almost to the root.

Genevieve loved this position, she decided. She leaned back a little so she could watch as his cock tunneled in and out of her, bathed in her wetness. When she glanced up, she found his gaze fixed on the apex of their legs as well, his expression tight and focused with concentration.

Needing more stimulation, she used her own hands to work her breasts, tugging the nipples in rhythm with her body screwing down upon him. She could feel his eyes watching her, and he groaned, his hips arching into her. Sensations exploded every time his hard cock thrust, hitting just the perfect spot with the thick head. The walls of her pussy rippled around him—gripping him and dragging when he withdrew, parting and sucking him back in.

His hips moved faster, and he grunted with every thrust, punctuating the slap of their bodies. "I'm sorry, baby. I don't think I can hold on," he panted. "You're so tight, so hot."

She mewled, struggling to get closer to him, her hands clenching on her breasts. She was so close, her orgasm just out of reach, bigger and more explosive than anything she had brought herself to or reached with a partner.

Not breaking the rhythm of his hips, he tucked his hand between their straining bodies, using a fingertip to rub her taut clitoris.

She went wild, crying out and raking her short nails down his chest as he rubbed and pinched and kept up the hammering of his cock inside of her. Her energy gathered over his invasion and finally imploded. She gave a fractured scream as the walls of her vagina clenched down on him and then subsided into rippling convulsions.

In her daze, she heard his roar of satisfaction before he plunged inside her to the hilt. His release spurted high inside her, and it triggered another small climax. He gave a low grunt as her walls milked his cock.

Warm and sweaty, she collapsed on top of him, her head buried in his neck. Long minutes passed before either of them moved. He turned his head and looked at her, his expression that of a man fully satiated. With the heat of mating past, a slight draft drifted over her body, raising goose bumps and teasing sensitive flesh. She shivered.

"Cold, angel?"

She shook her head, not trusting her voice to speak. The experience of being with him had been so intense, so over the top, she felt like someone had punched her in the solar plexus. Surely a fling wasn't supposed to feel like this?

Just as the doubt and fears and insecurities started

creeping over her, she felt his big hand pat her bottom as he yawned. "I'm going to take a quick little nap."

A simple plan formed in her mind: store up memories of some hot sex and good times with a hot, good man. Don't fall in love. Easy, right?

Chapter Nine

"'He held her close'…Alex, stop."

"What?"

"You're gnawing on my ear."

"I'm giving you love nibbles. Brock just did it."

Genevieve snorted and leaned away from his amorous mouth. "If Brock jumped off a cliff…"

"Man, I wish he'd jump off a cliff. That is one obnoxious guy."

"You're just mad I wouldn't let you pick the book with the anti-terrorist agent hero."

"Hell yeah. Now that would be awesome. Better than this pussy."

The other book had had a more erotic bent, which was why Genevieve had insisted on the sweeter historical. Though she had become at ease around Alex, narrating an erotic romance stretched outside her comfort bounds.

As Alex moved down her neck, she sighed and tilted her head to give him better access. Though he'd never admit it aloud, the sex yesterday afternoon had overexerted him; he'd been out cold for the better part of the night. They'd enjoyed some slumberous morning fun earlier today, but from the erection under her butt she knew he was ready to go again.

She sat on his lap in her large armchair, wrapped in a quilt. He'd remained naked after his shower this morning to give his washed boxers a chance to dry. Genevieve couldn't complain, since the view was so very nice.

"I think it stopped snowing."

Her heart seized a little, and she followed his gaze out the window. "That doesn't mean much. It's been going off and on for the past couple of days."

"True."

For a guy whose return to his normal life depended on the weather, Alex didn't sound like he cared much. In fact, she'd lost some of her urgency as well. Instead of checking the phone compulsively, she had just picked it up this morning once. She noted with some surprise that it was already Friday. How could he have fallen on her doorstep only five days ago?

Alex shifted her a bit so he could pick up the chipped mug on the small table next to the chair. He drank deeply and smacked his lips. "How come your hot chocolate tastes so good?"

"Told you, it's a secret ingredient."

"Whiskey?"

"Kind of. A shot of Bailey's and crème de menthe."

He gave a rumble of appreciation. "Here, last sip. You drink it."

"You can have it."

"No, it's so good. You barely had any."

She drank when he tipped the mug to her mouth, warmed by the drink and the simple gesture. She had the feeling that he would have drank a vat of the hot cocoa if she had it, but instead he made sure she enjoyed the last lingering taste.

When every drop was drained, he placed the mug back on

the table and kissed her gently, sharing the hint of chocolate and mint. Languor stole through her body. When their lips separated, she leaned against his chest, the book forgotten in her hands.

"You're a con artist. That's why you hate cops."

She smiled, used to his teasing and so relaxed she couldn't do anything but tease back. "Yes. I defrauded people of their millions and retired to a snowy cabin. Mexico is so passé."

"You're smart. You know no one will ever find you here." He shifted her hair aside, left down at his request, and pressed butterfly kisses against her neck.

"Alex," she said, only half-protesting. "I have chores to do."

"So pretend I'm a chore." He massaged her belly. In an instant, her baseline of relaxed arousal flared into full-blown, gimme-gimme-want-it-bad lust. "I'm kind of getting a bit of a complex, babe."

She hated being called a babe. *Got that, vagina? It's not a turn-on.* "About what?"

"You've been in the driver's seat when it comes to sex with us. I just want it clear, it's not always going to be like that."

"You make it sound like I dress up in black leather and carry a whip." At his silence, she twisted around. "Um, does that turn you on?"

"Of course not."

"Ooooh, yes it does," she teased, and nuzzled his neck. "That sounds like a fun fantasy. Maybe we can try that one out?"

He tilted his head farther back in silent acquiescence. Genevieve nibbled her way up to his jaw line, loving the way he smelled like her homemade soap and tasted so earthy, like a man. Mostly loving his shortened breath when he spoke.

"You in leather sounds awesome. You kind of have that Xena thing going on. Have you ever had a lesbian experience?"

Genevieve shook her head. Sometimes following his train of thought took some doing. "What?"

"You know, everyone thinks Xena and Gabrielle got it on. Not that I'm into girl on girl." He paused. "Much. Not obsessively at least."

"I have not had a girl-on-girl experience."

She kissed him and managed to shut him up for a second. When she came up for air, though, he spoke. "Would you want…?"

"I don't know how this went from me being a dominatrix to a lesbian fetish."

"It's not a fetish. I don't mind you being the bad dominatrix who I get to punish." He waggled his eyebrows.

"I think that defeats the whole purpose of me being a dominatrix."

"Well, I'm not into being tied down or anything."

Genevieve nibbled his earlobe between her teeth. "Now you're just giving me ideas."

She jumped with surprise when large hands closed on her hips, easily picking her up to turn her around. Within seconds, she found herself straddling his lap. "Don't strain your shoulder."

He made a dismissive noise. "I'm fine. If you only knew some of my ideas, sweetheart, you'd run screaming."

"Oh, yeah? Big, bad man. You forget how long I've had to fantasize."

"So, what do you want? Tell me."

She shouldn't have teased him. By the hard glint in his eyes, she was about to see the full force of his dominant personality. She couldn't wait. "I want your hands on me."

"Do you want me inside of you?"

His words turned her on as much as his touch. She nodded.

"Then say it. Say, 'Fuck me, Alex.'"

Her stomach knotted in arousal. "Fuck...me. Alex, please."

He cupped her face and smiled into her eyes. "I can get a bit rough in bed. If you want me to stop, just tell me and I will." He lowered his head to hers, his surprisingly soft lips brushing against hers.

He kissed her without demand, his hand coming up to cup her breast. It was sweet and pleasant, but she wanted a more aggressive touch as the heat built inside her. She tilted her head farther back and raised one hand to grip his hair. She tugged gently, and he seemed to approve of the slight pain. Alex gripped her jaw with one strong hand and turned her head forcefully to an angle he approved of, his tongue pushing past her lips. He thrust with his tongue, while his hand rubbed in a circular motion on her breast.

She tightened her legs and squeezed his thighs, but it didn't help much. Feeling bold, she captured his tongue on the next thrust and sucked on it.

He tore his mouth away from her, his eyes hot and narrowed with arousal. "Stand up."

She stood, facing him. His cock had completely hardened during their kiss. Alex sat back in the armchair and studied her from top to bottom. His body was long and rangy, the white bandage a sharp contrast to his dark skin. She attempted a wobbly smile. "I feel like a harem girl being surveyed by a sultan."

A streak of anticipation flitted through her as his eyes grew even hotter. "Well, now, sweetheart. How did you know that's one of *my* favorite fantasies?" He snapped his fingers. "But now that I think about it, harem girls are usually wearing a lot less clothes, aren't they? Strip down, baby." He relaxed into the chair, looking more tough and arrogant than any man had a right to. Knowing that his arrogance was tempered by the tenderness in his touch made it even more exciting.

She removed her sweater and jeans. She hesitated when she came to her bra and panties and stripped those off slowly.

"That's the prettiest thing I've ever seen," he murmured hoarsely, staring at her body with a worshipful expression. He looked at her face, which she was sure was red with arousal. "Touch yourself."

A bolt of surprise and interest shot through her. "In front of you?"

He smiled with wicked intent. "You want me to choose you for my bed, don't you? Show me why I should." Still she hesitated. "Are you disobeying me, Genevieve?" He raised an eyebrow. "Because if you are, I may just have to spank you."

She felt an instant rush of warmth between her legs at the seductive threat. There was a subtle question in his gaze, and she knew he would stop the game immediately if she wanted him to, but she didn't intend to do so. The sexual tension in the air seduced her.

She cupped her breasts with shaky hands, caressing the curves before capturing the nipples. She hadn't ever masturbated while standing, but having him watch her turned her on even if her hands didn't. She closed her eyes and moaned as she pinched her nipples before sliding her hands down her soft belly.

"Open your pussy," he whispered hoarsely. "Let me see you."

Teasing him, she slowly spread the lips of her labia apart, displaying the pouting pink flesh and the hard clitoris before dipping her fingers into the wetness and rubbing. She heard him groan and opened her eyes to see him stroking his hard shaft, pleasuring himself with no self-consciousness. The mesmerizing motion captured her eyes. She focused her attention on her clit, small ripples already beginning inside of her. His hand captured her wrist, stilling her motion.

"No," he said curtly. "I want you to come with my cock inside of you."

Small shivers of arousal wracked her body, and he didn't miss a single one. "Look at you, baby. You're ready to go, and I haven't even touched you." He sighed, shaking his head in mock regret. "It's too bad I need a little more preparation."

Preparation? He was so aroused he practically vibrated, his penis curving up toward his bellybutton.

When he pulled her closer and tugged her down, she got an inkling of what he was looking for.

With a small smile and a flirtatious glance under her lashes, she responded to the pressure and sank to her knees at his feet, her body feeling a fresh flush of arousal at the thought of performing this sexual act with him.

She grasped his cock at the base and angled it toward her mouth, struck anew at how intimidating he was. She brushed a fleeting kiss across the plump head and then licked the vein running up the bottom. He sifted through her hair before tangling his fingers in the strands. She raised a brow in mock innocence.

"Stop teasing me, baby," he whispered hoarsely. "Suck it now."

She kept her gaze locked on his as she engulfed the broad head in her mouth. He was so thick her fingers barely touched

119

where she encircled him, and her lips felt stretched. He tasted delicious, earthy and salty and exactly as she thought a man should taste. She experimented with small dips of her head until his fingers became more insistent in her hair. He pulled her forward, pushing into her mouth with a slow, measured thrust of his hips.

"Shit, you're so sweet. You don't know how hot it makes me to see your lips part for me," he rasped. His hips withdrew and thrust again, a little bit harder. She whimpered and took his passion, loving the dazed vulnerability and pleasure in his brown eyes.

Alex had died and gone to Heaven. But he was sure angels had nothing on Genevieve.

It wasn't the first blowjob he'd gotten but, by God, even with her hesitancy and inexperience, he didn't think he'd ever had better. The sight alone drove him crazy, those eyes glancing up at him boldly, her pouty lips stretched wide over his cock. She was so damned generous, taking his thrusts easily, her hands rubbing the flesh her lips couldn't reach, her tongue stroking over the tip of him on each pass.

He tightened his hands in her hair, tugging on the strands. His lust flared hotter at the small moan she gave. Oh yes, she was the perfect match for him—he loved a woman who liked her hair pulled. He was ready to stop at a moment's notice if it got too much for her, but so far she hadn't complained, thank God.

"You like that, don't you? Suck me harder." He tugged at her hair again. She made an agreeable sound and mouthed the sensitive head of his dick, taking his pleasure to a whole new level.

His thrusts came harder and shorter...he could feel his balls tightening, the tingling in his spine. He cupped her face and tried to pull her head away. "Back up, baby. I'm going to come."

She moaned in acceptance, her head dipping lower, resisting his attempts to pull her off.

He slid his fingers inside of her mouth to pry her off, but she held on, flattening her tongue and taking him almost to the back of her throat on the next thrust, swallowing around him, milking him. That was all it took. He jerked in the chair, holding her head to him, and erupted in her mouth, one pulsating jet after another. She made a startled noise, but held on, taking his passion inside of her.

He collapsed in the chair as she sat back on her knees and wiped her mouth. Looking at her naked body, her mussed hair and her lips shiny wet from her mouth and his come, he hardened again to readiness. She was violently aroused, her eyes dazed and hot, small shivers coursing through her. He held out his hand. "Come here and sit on me."

She rose in an unsteady movement and straddled him. His cock flirted with the entrance to her body, just pushing inside of the silky wet folds. At the hot kiss, his hands clenched on her hips. "Take me in, Genevieve. I'm going to die if I don't get inside of you again."

"Wait, let me do it," she said coyly, capturing the insistent hands on her hips. Still she teased him, only allowing half of his size inside of her before lifting. He held his breath as the tip of him came close to withdrawing before she lowered herself again, walls of tight wetness just grasping and releasing the head of his dick.

It wasn't nearly enough. "Deeper, Genevieve. Take it now," he growled.

"You don't like this?" she asked slyly as she dipped a little lower.

Oh God, he loved her natural sexuality. His fingers bit into her hips as he gave her a mock frown. "You're not behaving, Genevieve."

She laughed, a free, joyful sound. "I'm really scared, Alex." She gasped as he leaned forward to capture her nipple between his teeth, giving it a quick, careful bite.

He laved the nipple and smiled at her threateningly. "You should be." He opened his hand and carefully slapped her ass, not hard, mindful of her delicate flesh, just a light swat to nudge her burning up a notch.

She squealed with outrage, but he could see the flare of arousal in her eyes, the tightening and rush of cream on his dick where she gripped just the tip. "You hit me!"

"No, I tapped you." He smacked her other cheek and she moaned. "I'll spank you harder if you disobey me again. Take all of me."

Her eyes were dark amethyst and hot as she stared at him. He realized that the amulet she wore between her full breasts had changed colors, darkened to the exact shade of her eyes. She licked her lips and then deliberately lifted herself up, completely off his dick. The air felt cold and unpleasant as it rushed over him, but did nothing to dull the hot blood flowing through him at the level of trust she'd just handed to him.

He growled and jerked her flush against him for a bruising kiss, no longer gentle, eating at her lips. He held her head still for the dominant thrust of his tongue while his other hand slid down her body to cup her ass. She screamed into his mouth as he tapped her rounded butt a half a dozen times, each slap vibrating on the flesh of his cock held against her. When he knew her ass would be blushing he brought his hand down between the crease and filled her pussy with three fingers, making her cry out in pleasure and relief. She was dripping down her thighs and over his hand.

"Please, Alex, I need you," she mewled.

"What do you need? My cock?"

"Oh yes, please."

"So polite," he murmured with a dark smile. He held her tight to him and turned them in the chair so she was sitting. He arranged her legs over the armrests, bent his knees and thrust into her to the hilt. She came immediately, and he gritted his teeth as he felt the tight contractions on his dick.

He shafted her in deep strokes, his balls slapping against her sex on every thrust, keeping her orgasm alive. It became one long episode of shivers and contractions. A dull throb in his right arm increased with every stroke, protesting the strain of the position, but he couldn't stop. He knew he should have been able to hold out much longer after his earlier release, but the feeling of her writhing underneath him, her body soft and flushed, her moans loud and uninhibited, stripped his control away. He hammered into her until he erupted, feeling as though his orgasm came from the soles of his feet.

He caught himself before he could collapse on her heaving body and found the energy to haul her up and reverse their positions until she draped his chest.

"Alex," she gasped, raising her head. "Your injury. You shouldn't have done that."

"Tired of being on the bottom. 'S'okay." She fumbled with the bandage but he caught her hand. "Everything's fine." His shoulder and arm ached like a son of a bitch, but the wound hadn't bled or opened. It could wait.

She apparently didn't think so, though, and wriggled and wiggled until he allowed her to peel off the gauze and poke and prod him with knowledgeable fingers, tsking under her breath.

Alex found himself smiling at her fussiness, warmed by her worry and concern. His mother would love Genevieve.

He didn't think he had ever voluntarily brought a woman home to meet his mother, who was a nice lady but one determined to see her eldest son married and settled. But now he'd met a mysterious woman laden with secrets and seemingly more commitment-shy than him on his worst day. And all he could imagine was taking her out to enjoy Sunday brunch and a game of Parcheesi with the fam.

And then maybe a chick flick, just to make her happy. Something with Matthew McConaughey.

Alex barely restrained a full body shudder.

Okay, so they might have to skip the movie. But keeping her happy? That he actually could see himself trying to do. He was in way deeper than he had anticipated. He'd crashed, burned, and he wouldn't be able to get out of this, wouldn't be able to leave her with his heart intact. He'd never thought he would be able to just fuck her and go, and now he was sure of it. His mind worked at lightning speed, as if he was on another high-profile case. But in this case the perp he needed to nail was Genevieve's heart and trust.

She is yours. You are hers.

Yes, Papa.

He'd somehow forgotten his father's words to him as he lay near death, but now they bloomed in his mind. Call it magic, call it fate, but he couldn't believe the two of them weren't meant for one another.

To distract himself from his heavy thoughts and her from her role as his doctor, he slipped his hand under her and drove two fingers straight into her channel, softened and slippery from their earlier play. She gasped and froze, her hand just finishing moving the bandage back into place.

"You only came once. I came twice."

She shuddered as he started a driving rhythm, her head falling back, her hips moving in time with him. "It's not a contest."

His laugh was genuine and rife with sensual promise. "You're right. I win either way."

Chapter Ten

"Admit it. This was all an evil plot to kill me, wasn't it?"

Genevieve smiled at the rough voice rumbling above her. She lay with her head on his chest, studying the light creeping into the cabin from under the curtains. Her body actually hurt from the fun they'd had all night.

"Why do you say that?"

"I was doing great, on the road to mending, and then you decided to lay me flat with some superb sex."

Though her chest puffed at that admission of "superb", she encountered a small pang of regret. "Are you okay? We probably shouldn't have overdone…" She raised her head, but he pressed it back down.

"Stop fretting. I'm fine." He yawned, a jaw-cracking noise. "Just tired. Let's sleep a bit before the next round, okay?"

He could sleep. She was too filled with nervous energy. She snuggled close until she heard his breathing even out and then separated their naked limbs from one another. Genevieve looked down at him, sleep relaxing his hard features until he appeared much younger than he was.

The bruises on his face were gone, the cuts just angry scars. They would fade in a few days, as well. Genevieve couldn't help the surge of pride that soared through her at the sight.

She'd never attempted to use her gift on such a large-scale healing, and the possibilities it opened were endless. Maybe she could help other people too.

Helping people means you have to leave here. Are you ready for that? Genevieve shuddered. No, she didn't know if she could leave.

She'd only done penance for two years. Was two years enough time to pay for killing someone?

Absolutely not. It was all his fault, making her think such things about leaving here and the future and happiness. She didn't deserve any of that.

This was just what it was, a grab at some fleeting joy. The years stretched ahead of her, and she needed some small spurts of pleasure to hold her through it, that was all. Even prisoners had music and books and the occasional conjugal visit to keep them sane.

She eased from the bed, wincing a bit at the protest of her leg muscles. God, she needed a shower. Alex hadn't seemed to mind his scent on her, but she wasn't used to being marked by someone else.

When she emerged from the shower, Alex was still fast asleep, so after doing her daily check of the still-dead phone, she decided to go outside. Her horse, Barney, was used to eating at the exact same time every day. It wasn't good for a horse's digestion to have the time vary from day to day. Unfortunately, since Alex had come, she'd had to time her slipping out to coincide with his naps. One, because he was fun to hang out with while he was awake, and two, because she figured he would shit the proverbial brick if he knew she was wandering around outside.

Not that she was scared of him, Genevieve hastened to

127

reassure herself. But why worry him if it was unnecessary?

The sun was out, so bright it hurt her eyes where it shined against the snow. As Alex had noted yesterday, the snow had stopped falling. She hadn't listened to the radio yet, but no doubt the roads were on their way to being plowed out. Soon her telephone service would be restored. Since Alex was almost back up to speed, in another day or two, one way or another, he'd be on his way home. Genevieve rubbed at her chest. God, why did that hurt so much?

She entered her ramshackle barn and leaned her shotgun up against the outside of Barney's stall. "Hey, buddy."

He answered her with a whinny and she smiled. Now this she understood. Her animals had become her friends over the past few years, a silent sounding-board for her worries and problems. *You're starting to sound like a demented Disney princess.*

Genevieve winced. Okay, maybe she'd become as weird as the gossips made her out to be. Alex had reminded her how nice it was to talk to someone who talked back. Though she had to say, she'd never enjoyed the company of any of her friends the way she enjoyed his...

Drop it.

She sighed as she finished taking care of Barney and closed the stall. She needed to stop mooning over the guy. As she left the barn and started trekking through the snow back to the house, she contemplated if that was even a possibility. Maybe they could have a sexual marathon for the rest of the day. She could work him out of her system a little faster.

Genevieve was so caught up in imagining the new sexual positions they could try out that her mind didn't quite grasp the sharp crack that rang through the air. It was only as she felt the whiz of the bullet near her ear that she comprehended someone was shooting at her.

Though adrenaline pulsed through her body, her mind remained collected as she swiftly calculated the distance between her and the two buildings. Since the cabin was closer, she ran full tilt toward it, conscious of the bullets spraying the ground behind her feet. The sound of the gunshots was obscenely loud in the still winter morning.

When she was about four feet away from the house she heard Alex roar her name, and for the first time, pure panic flooded through her. Oh God, no, he couldn't come outside, he could get shot. When the door opened and Alex ran out into the sun, she put on a burst of speed, hurtling through the door and right into him. She kicked the door closed and dragged them both to the floor. "Get down, get down!"

"Genevieve, what the hell..."

They were both breathing hard, her from her flight, him, presumably, from fear. "Someone shot at me."

"I could hear that." His arms were trembling as they wrapped around her. Taking her by surprise, he rolled them over until his body lay over hers. He was protecting her, she realized. "Were the bullets coming from just one direction?"

"I-I don't know. I just wanted to get away."

He squeezed her. "Okay. Stay here."

He rose on his knees, and Genevieve dimly grasped that he was still completely naked. "What are you going to do?"

"I just want to see if I can see anything out the window. Give me the gun."

She became conscious of her fingers locked tightly around the gun barrel. She'd forgotten she even carried it. Responding to the command in his voice, she almost handed it right over before she pulled back. "Wait. That's stupid. The shots have stopped. Don't give the guy a target."

"I have to look."

He pulled the gun from her hand and stayed low to the ground as he moved over to one of the windows. He flicked the curtain aside and peered out.

It took Genevieve a couple of seconds before she understood she was just lying on the ground like a damsel in distress. She firmed her jaw and crawled over to the opposite window.

"Get the hell down and away from the window."

"I'll do it when you do." She looked out the window, following his example and keeping her body angled away. She was struck by a strong sense of déjà vu, as she was recreating her exact position when she'd found Alex.

She had a feeling she wouldn't be coming across a hunky guy in need right now, though.

The front yard was ominously silent and empty. A rustle of the trees on the west side caught her eye and she glanced quickly to see a flash of silver and a glimpse of something tan. "Did you see that? Over there, to the left."

Alex went stock-still and they both sat in strained silence. Nothing moved. Shaken, Genevieve turned to Alex. His expression was frozen, intense, but he couldn't hide the paleness of his face or the sweat popping out on his brow.

Between the sex they'd shared and the way she'd just body slammed him to the ground, he was going to be hurting a bit. "Alex, go lie down. I'll keep watch."

"I'm not letting a woman stand guard over me while I do nothing."

"That's stupid."

"I'm not tired."

"Alex—"

"Shut up, Genevieve."

She was so startled at the harshness of his tone, she jumped. He took one look at her and gave a rough sigh, scraping his hand through his hair. "I'm sorry, sweetheart. Can you stay close to the ground and check the phone?"

Since she'd been dying to anyway, she crawled over to the phone. Sure enough, the dial tone was still missing. "It's dead. Do you think this is the guy who shot you?"

"What are the odds that there are two lunatics with guns running around?"

"Do you have any enemies?"

"Every policeman who does his job properly has enemies. Do any come straight to mind? No. I left my violent work in New York. I've been pushing paper around down here, damn it." He shook his head. "You're sure the shortwave doesn't work?"

"No. Unless you're mechanically oriented and want to try your hand at it." Christ, everything that had kept Alex with her took on a sinister glow now. Just think, she'd been bemoaning the fact that the phones would soon be restored.

"I hand in my man card when it comes to fixing appliances. Okay, how much more ammo do you have?"

"A few boxes in the closet, in the back."

"You stay here with the gun, keep an eye out. I'm going to move it in here. We can barricade ourselves in for the most part."

It didn't take him long to haul the ammunition back inside the main room. The supply, which she'd figured only a couple of weeks ago was more than sufficient, looked pitifully low when it was gathered together. He had a pair of ratty-looking grey sweatpants and a pair of huge sneakers in the pile, which she frowned at. "Where did you get those?"

"There's a box at the top of your closet." Standing out of direct line of either of the windows, he stepped into the sweatpants. Whoever had worn them before must have been significantly shorter and smaller than Alex. The hem barely reached his ankles, and the cotton clung lovingly to his ass. "They aren't the best fit and the shoes look huge, but if we need to make a break for it, I have to be covered."

Desperation welled at his words. Where would they make a break for it? There was no one nearby they could run to. When he was stationed in front of the window farthest from the door again, Genevieve crept to her bedside table and withdrew her .22. She brought the handgun to him. "Here. You can use this."

He didn't look surprised. "I wondered why you had bullets in this caliber. Good. I'm more at ease with this than the shotgun." He opened the window slightly. Just enough to stick the barrel of the gun out, she noted. She did the same on the opposite window.

"I tinted the windows last year to keep the summer sun from baking me. If we keep to the side, someone looking in may not be able to really see inside."

"Well, that's something in our favor."

She tried to lighten the mood. "Hey, at least I have the police chief in my pocket. I mean, could I get more luck than to get stranded in a shootout with a lawman? And look, he's not even shooting."

As if her words were the impetus, a volley of shots rang forth, peppering the building. She and Alex ducked. Thank God, none of the bullets hit either of the windows. The logs could take it, glass couldn't. She sat up, ready to shoot back, but he stayed her actions. "No. Don't shoot him unless you have a clear target. We have a limited amount of bullets. As far as we know, he's got a whole jeep full."

They both peered out the window as the gunfire stopped. Nothing was visible. "He's playing with us." Genevieve wasn't sure if Alex was speaking to her or himself.

He turned around to sit with his back against the wall, the gun cradled across his lap. He was beyond pale. "We're stuck in here."

"You've exhausted yourself."

Alex rested his head against the wall and closed his eyes. "I don't think I've ever been that terrified in my life as I was when I heard those shots and realized you weren't inside. It brought back some bad memories."

It was on the tip of her tongue to apologize, but he opened his eyes and pinned her with a hard gaze. "Can I ask what you were doing outside when I specifically said you shouldn't leave the cabin until I was better?" His tone was soft, but it did nothing to hide his anger.

Genevieve reminded herself that she was a fully independent grown woman and should not be intimidated by such obvious tactics. "Um, feeding the animals?" Oh wonderful. Nothing screamed strong and brave better than an "Um" and a question mark at the end of a statement. She cleared her throat. "Feeding the animals."

His scowl turned blacker. "Animals. Outside. Alone. When we know there's a shooter on the loose. Brilliant, Genevieve."

Okay, so it hadn't been the smartest move, but she really hadn't had a choice. "Just so we're clear, I don't like your tone. I've been careful and I've been going outside alone the whole time you've been here—I'm sorry if you happened to wake up this time, but my chores aren't going to do themselves just because I have a cranky guest." Oh, probably not a good idea to tell him he had slept through her slipping outside, she realized as the muscles in his jaw bunched. But really, what was she supposed to do? She hated being vulnerable, but someone had to tend the horse and everything else. She tried to go on the defensive to deflect the obvious lecture he was gearing up for. "And, in my defense, I had no idea someone was trying to actively gun you down. What are the odds?"

He spoke through gritted teeth. "It's common sense to not make a target of yourself if you can avoid it. Any crazy could take it in their head to come out here and hurt you. You could have just asked me to come along. I can protect you. I can do this stuff for you. You shouldn't be here alone, you should be..."

"I should be what?"

"I don't know!" Alex shouted, startling her. Genuine concern and worry was written all over his face. "You should be inside. You should let me take care of you."

"And what am I going to do when you leave?" she asked quietly.

His mouth gaped. "You really think I was just going to walk away from you?"

"Why not?"

"And you could walk away from me."

"Sure."

He snorted. "So you're telling me I'm nothing but a piece of meat to you? Seriously? You weren't scared for my well-being at all when bullets were flying out there."

She'd been terrified at the thought that he might get hit. "I'd be worried for any human."

His eyes grew flinty. "You're lying."

She shivered. It was like a cold draft had brushed through the room. Though she was glad they were having the conversation, this wasn't really the appropriate time.

Nonetheless, she pushed out the vile words on her tongue. "I'm not quite sure why you're not understanding this," she said deliberately. "When we're done here, when you go back to town—that's it. To me, you're no different from any other man who could have wound up here. I want to not be shot, maybe get some more fucking, and then I want you to leave as soon as you are physically able. Is that clear?"

His face had hardened during her words, but he flinched at the obscenity. His lips barely moved when he spoke. "Perfectly."

Her stomach literally cramped, and she wanted to scrub her mouth with lye for demeaning what they had shared. "Good. We need some sort of plan."

He wouldn't look at her. "We're stuck here until the phone comes back online. We can't exactly jump on a horse and go galloping off into the open. We'll be sitting ducks. In the meantime, I can keep watch."

"We'll take turns."

"Fine."

She leaned her head against the wall, staring out the window. "Fine."

"Did you hear something?"

"It was the wind."

"Oh." Genevieve turned back to the book in her hands. She'd curled up on the floor next to the chair, a big mistake since it reminded her of their tumultuous lovemaking, and tried to take her mind off their mutual problem.

She reread the page she was on, but gave up after the second sentence blurred. She set it facedown in her lap and did her best to pretend she wasn't studying her protector.

Despite his coldness all day, that's exactly what he'd set himself up to be. He sat propped up against the wall, the handgun clenched in his hand, peering out the window. Except for a quick trip to the bathroom, he hadn't moved.

The tension of their careful politeness and distance added to the stress of the horrible situation they were in. Genevieve had an idea of what civilians in war-torn countries might feel like. Every so often, a volley of gunshots peppered the sturdy cabin from the front, bouncing off the logs. None had penetrated the two windows yet, but it was only a matter of time. They had taken to crawling along the floor if they needed to move, to avoid any stray bullets.

Alex had fired just a few times, when he thought he had a bead on the guy. Though he had curtly mentioned it sounded like there was only one shooter, as the shots were coming from one direction, he said the guy was too deep in the woods to see him. He didn't want to waste their ammunition. Plus, he said the guy might get stupid if he thought they didn't have much in the way of weapons.

It was a smart plan, though Genevieve's first instinct was to go in with guns blazing. He was right though; the shooter had a number of places to hide while they had none.

They hadn't spoken much, whatever conversation they had stilted and tense. Genevieve was aware he was mad. Meanwhile, she wanted to cut out her own tongue for what she'd said to him. Deep down, she knew she hadn't just wounded his pride. The man was sweet and tender, and more than a little romantic. It seemed as though he'd really fallen for the person he thought she was. He had no idea though. It was best this way, best to make a clean break.

So why did she hurt so much too?

She licked her lips and ventured some conversation into the silence. "It's been quiet. What do you think the guy's plan is?"

He rested his head against the wall. "I don't know. Can you check the phone?"

They'd been checking every hour, and though she was certain it wouldn't do any good now, she checked again anyway. "Dead." She walked hunched over to the fridge and removed her pitcher of iced tea. "Do you want something to drink?"

"I'm fine, thanks."

His politeness was grating and she straightened, out of direct range of the windows. With more force than she intended, she set her glass on the counter and filled it up, then drank it in a few gulps.

"I hope Barney's okay." The stray thought slipped out of her mouth. She'd gotten too used to talking to Alex. It seemed natural to blurt out her worries.

"The horse?"

"Yeah."

"I'm sure he's fine."

His tone didn't invite any further conversation, but still she tried. "I wish I could check on him. What if he's—?"

"You are not going outside."

She had no intention of waltzing outside, but his command scraped along her independent soul. Genevieve glared at him. He returned her gaze, the remoteness in his face chilling her. "I'd appreciate it, as a favor to the man you're currently fucking, if you'd promise me to exercise some caution for the remainder of our time together. After this is over, you can do whatever you want with all the other lunatics with guns running amok down here. Hell, maybe one of them can even service you when I'm gone."

Oh, ouch. Having words thrown back in your face was never a good thing, and Genevieve acknowledged the hit with only a slight flinch. If he expected her to fly into a rage or burst into tears, he was going to be surprised. She was almost relieved the other shoe had dropped. What could she say? She was a fair person, and the first to admit she deserved much, much worse than a snide comment in response to her childish behavior and words.

He was still watching her, but she didn't really know what else to say. She wasn't about to engage and make this more of a farce. So she returned to her place by the armchair and picked up her book.

Her eyesight blurred, the words dancing in front of her. She frowned and looked up. Her breath caught. Alex's physical form had become buried under layers of colors. Holy crap, had her full powers returned?

She couldn't ignore the tempting lure of his aura and she bathed in it. The arousal at the topmost level was easily brushed aside. She didn't need to see his aura to know that he wanted her, though it was nice to have some proof of how deep his lust went. The hurt underneath it tugged her heartstrings. The pink of his injuries was expected, and she gave it a cursory glance, relieved to see that it looked very faint. To experiment, she gave a few tugs at that layer in critical areas she felt may help him. The pink flared purple for a second. She heard and felt his physical body flinch.

But it was the base layer that called to her. When she reached it, her breath just about stopped.

Christ, blue. It was so damn blue. She'd never seen anything so beautiful and clear. She wanted to roll herself up in his soul, bathe in its beauty.

And he had called her an angel? According to this, he was about two steps away from serious wings. Purity had nothing to do with sexual matters or prayer. It was the basic, bone-deep soul a person was born with. Alex was so pure, her eyes were hurting.

Her instincts had been dead on. Unless she was reading him wrong, and she'd never read anyone wrong, this was one hell of a man. She felt...a bit humbled, frankly, that he had wanted her to the degree that he did.

And he was hers. There was no getting around the way her brain was clamoring for what she was seeing right now. Whether she was worthy of him or not...holy crap, what had she thrown away?

As quickly as it had come, the colors vanished, and she had to blink to bring the here and now back into focus. Everything looked dull and washed out after that little acid trip.

Well. Now she certainly had some thinking to do.

Chapter Eleven

Genevieve wasn't going to be sleeping tonight. Alex didn't blame her, he was uptight as well. They'd pushed the mattress up against the wall farthest from the windows, right next to the frame of the bed. It was just an illusion of safety, Alex knew. She was sitting on the mattress, scribbling something into a notebook.

The sex from last night, combined with the adrenaline-pumping terror of Genevieve in danger, had just about wiped him out physically. When he'd heard that gunshot, he'd gotten a heavy dose of the PTSD that had kept him from returning to work after Jerry'd been killed. He'd frozen, completely useless for a critical minute. It could have cost Genevieve her life.

A showdown might very well come to a head pretty soon, so he needed to rest. With the phones out, they had no way of calling for help. Sure, if someone had managed to make it up the roads to them, perhaps the police weren't far behind but that meant his search party had to a) still be looking for him and b) looking in the right place.

He was getting too old for this crap.

Alex pursed his lips, his gaze drawn to Genevieve. He was still smarting over her words from earlier. The fact that it was her defense mechanism didn't matter. Combined with his terror, the things she'd said had triggered his, *oh yeah, well screw you* reflex.

For the past few hours he'd been sitting here trying to list every single one of her damn faults.

One, she was secretive as hell.

Maybe she has a reason for it.

Two, she was prickly to the point of being irritating.

You like her sassiness. She's not prickly in bed.

Three, the things she'd said had hurt him.

You're a pussy. Your expectations that she would fall in love with you in the space of a week are ridiculous.

Yeah, but the kicker was, he'd fallen for her, hard. Alex had never been a big believer in love at first sight. But with Genevieve the impossible became possible. If something as magical as her powers could exist, the entire universe opened up, a blank slate of anything goes.

Something bigger than both of them must be out there, something that had brought him to her. He'd never thought of himself as a romantic, but when he'd seen her, he'd known they were meant to be together.

Unfortunately, she clearly didn't feel the same way. Alex leaned his head against the wall, looking into the darkness. His heart ached at the thought of never seeing Genevieve again.

Of course, he'd take never seeing her again if he knew she was alive and safe somewhere in the world. They were in such a dire situation here, a recovering invalid and a young woman against a trigger-happy gunman. Not good.

As if she heard his thoughts, Genevieve stirred. He spared a glance to find her reaching under the frame of her bed and withdrawing a large box of some sort. They'd left only one candle burning, in an attempt to keep their visible silhouettes to a minimum, so he couldn't see very clearly. As tempted as he was to ask her what the box was, his pride had him keeping silent. Let her tell him if she wanted to. He didn't need the scraps.

Nonetheless, his heart sped and his ears perked up when she crawled over to where he sat. "Why aren't you sleeping?"

"I just realized I could die pretty soon."

His heart seized, the thin layer of ice he'd drawn around himself cracking at her pragmatic announcement. "The hell you will." Even if Genevieve didn't return his love, he'd be damned if he lost her. No matter what he had to do.

"I'm not stupid. Anyway, I don't have a will or anything. So I wrote down what I want, and I'd like you to sign it as a witness. I don't know how legal that is, but I figure it's better than nothing. Just in case, I'm going to tell you too."

Like a child, he wanted to plug his fingers in his ears and hum. "Please don't tell me this."

Her hand rested on his arm. A little zing of warmth flooded into his system. How could she not feel as intensely about him as he did about her? "I have to. This is important. I spread my mom's ashes around this place."

He focused on the outdoor landscape. "You want the same thing?"

"No."

The word was so emphatic, he couldn't help but look at her. Her eyes shone in the darkness, the whites very visible. "I don't want to be anywhere near here after I die. I don't care what happens with my ashes, but I don't want them here."

"Why do you live here if you hate it?"

Instead of telling him off for asking her a personal question, she smiled slightly. To his surprise, she answered. "Penance." Before he could ask her to elaborate, she opened the box in her hands. "These things are important to me, and I've written there that I want them cremated with me."

He didn't speak, though his curiosity was itching. As if she knew, she picked up the item on top. It was a small rag doll, the kind women used to make by hand. His mother had one of them from her own childhood stored away somewhere. Genevieve's doll was missing an eye and wore a faded terrycloth dress. "This was the doll I carried around when I was little. Her name's Betty Lou. When I was seven, I accidentally bleached her dress and cried because I was sure she wouldn't be pretty anymore. So Mom made a new one out of an old towel. She said she would buy me a new doll when we went to town, but I loved this one so much, I wouldn't let her."

She placed the doll gently back in the box. She held up a pressed flower encased in plastic. "This was the first rose I ever saw, when I was five. My mom said I carried it around in my pocket because I thought it was the most beautiful thing I'd ever seen. She planted rosebushes in the backyard for me, but after she died, I guess I didn't take care of them right, 'cause they all died."

Next, Genevieve stroked her fingers over a folded-up swatch of material. "My mother had to sell my grandma's wedding dress. I wasn't born yet. But she cut off a tiny scrap so I would have something of it."

Tears were streaming down Genevieve's cheeks, but she didn't seem to realize. Alex noticed, though, and his heart was breaking. "It sounds as though she loved you a lot. You should speak of her more often, honor that love."

"You don't even know how much she loved me." She withdrew a piece of paper from the bottom of the box. "This is the last picture I have of her."

The Polaroid showed an older woman who looked

remarkably like Genevieve, only more frail, her eyes sunken, her hair thinning. She sat on a knitted blanket outside. The woman in the photo stared at the photographer with a tenderness that shone through the print and brought a lump to his throat. Thin and wasted, she had the same look his grandmother had worn in the final stages of Alzheimer's, a kind of resignation and helplessness that conveyed death was near. "She's as beautiful as you." Alex passed the photo back to Genevieve, who lowered it with reverence back to the box. The click of the lid closing was very loud in the silent room.

She cleared her throat and handed the notebook and pen over to him. "Can you sign this, please?"

As much as he hated the idea, Alex couldn't deny the woman anything, and he signed before he glanced over the document. Besides her post-death wishes, which he still couldn't even begin to consider, she'd also listed a quick rundown of her assets, which were pitifully bare; the cabin and a bank account, which she had left to some man, a friend, Alex remembered her telling him about, and her horse, which she left to...

"You want to leave me your horse?"

"And money for his upkeep."

Ahh, yes, he saw that as well. "Why are you leaving me your horse?" Forget the fact that if she died, he didn't think he'd be alive. God as his witness, the only way she wouldn't be alive was if someone shot through him first.

Her eyes were shadowed, her gaze steady. "I don't care about the cabin or the money in my account. I love my horse."

His poor brain tried to make sense of her convoluted female logic, but he was tired and strung out. Fortunately, she continued to speak. "I didn't mean what I said earlier. I'm sorry, and I want to apologize."

His heart melted. "It's fine. Don't worry about it. You were tense."

"It wasn't nice. The truth is, if I had met you a few years ago, I would have said you were my dream man. You're so perfect and gentle and kind."

As nice as it sounded he had to interject. "I'm hardly perfect. You want to know why I was in such a bad mood? 'Cause I'm terrified I won't be able to protect you."

She paused. "What?"

"When you said you were lucky because you had me here...I'm no one you want on your team. After my partner died, the reason I couldn't return to work was because of the flashbacks. Hell, I could barely leave my apartment. I'd hear a car backfiring, or hear someone who sounded the slightest bit like Jerry, and I'd crumble."

"Post-traumatic stress disorder," she murmured.

"Yeah. Only I knew I couldn't get diagnosed, or I'd have a tough time working anywhere in law enforcement. So I pretended I was okay, faked my way through therapy and my brother did his best to find me a job where I wouldn't have to deal with anything that would set me off."

He knew that the shame he felt was written all over his face. "I really thought I was getting better. But when I heard those gunshots outside? I froze. Flat-out froze, even though I knew you must be out there and in danger."

"That's understandable."

"No. It's not. What kind of a cop am I? Hell, what kind of a man am I?"

"I think you're a very good man. Look at you. You aren't cowering under the bed, are you?"

He forced himself to admit the truth that cut into the very

base of his machismo. "I'm scared."

"You'd be stupid not to be. The fact that you're still willing and ready to face gunfire when you've got a mental block against it means that you're far braver than you're letting yourself believe you are." She hesitated. "Trust me when I say this; you don't have the soul of a coward or a weakling. I can see it."

Alex blinked. "What?"

"Your aura. It's beautiful. Except for my mother, I've never seen one like it."

He was startled. "You can see auras? You didn't mention that."

"I haven't done it in a long time. I didn't think I was able to until tonight."

Huh. He glanced down at himself, half expecting to see something floating around his body. "Does it mean I'm surrounded by a bunch of colors?"

"Something like that. It's a bit more complex, but it's tough to explain. Anyway, you have the soul of a natural-born caretaker." She shook her head. "You know, I hate to be so blunt..."

"Why stop now?"

"Ha-ha. Anyway, have you ever thought of getting out of law enforcement?"

He shook his head. "All my life, all I ever wanted to be was like my father. I'm never going to be a hero like him, but I don't know what else to do if I'm not a cop."

"Well, whatever. Rest assured, I know for a fact how good you are. You have nothing to be ashamed of. Trust me when I say that in this relationship, the problem isn't with you, it's with me. I'm the reason it would never work out."

"Genevieve..."

She surprised him by hugging him. "You tempt me. God, I want nothing more than to be with you."

"Sweetheart, there's no way you can make me believe that I'm any better than—"

She gave a short laugh. "You have no idea. Please, just hold me for a while."

Not quite sure what else to do or say, he tugged her closer and did just that.

Chapter Twelve

They sat quietly for another couple of hours, holding one another. Not a single gunshot broke the silence, and Genevieve drifted off to sleep.

She awoke to his hand idly stroking her hair. For a split-second, she forgot about the danger beyond the cabin walls, stretching languidly against him. When she looked up to find him gazing outside, reality crashed down on her. Glancing at her wristwatch, she saw it was already four in the morning. She hadn't meant to fall asleep. With the focus in his expression, Genevieve knew Alex hadn't slept so much as a wink.

"Why don't you sleep? I'll take watch," she said quietly.

He opened his mouth to argue, but then seemed to think again, which told her how tired he was. This was the first day since he'd been injured he'd gone more than five hours without catching a nap. She figured that he would fall into a deep sleep, and he didn't disappoint.

Genevieve took his place against the window and kept her attention on the darkness, the shotgun balanced in her lap. The shooter had been conspicuously silent for the past few hours. It was too much to hope he was gone.

Dying had never really bothered her before. When a person had no one left around to care, dying was really just a full stop at the end of a life.

She had Alex now, though. Despite her best efforts to keep her distance, she cared for him. She cared for him so much, if it was a matter of one of them surviving the night, she hoped it was him. The world would be a worse place without souls like his moving around on it. She couldn't see her own aura, but she was sure it couldn't possibly look anything like his. After what she'd done in her life, she must have badly tarnished it. No, there was no comparison. Plus, he had a mother and brother who cared for him.

She'd hatched a plan as soon as she'd realized her full powers had returned. Their conversation had cemented it. She had to protect Alex.

With his aura, she was a bit surprised by how long he'd managed to stay in law enforcement in such a dangerous area. It was like his soul was too pure for day-to-day violence. Her on the other hand...well, she didn't love violence. But she was a pragmatic person with a good plan on how to fix this. Her lover would never agree to it if she gave him a choice. So it was time for some sneaking.

She rested her gun against the wall as she crept to the coatrack to pull on her big coat. Her boots came on next. No need to be uncomfortable in the cold.

She looked out the window again and allowed her vision to blur and flip. Seeing an aura wasn't quite like thermal goggles, but it was all energy in the end. She couldn't see it through trees, alas, so if he was camped out deeper in the forest, she was shit out of luck.

Really, her best bet was to try this right after the jerk launched a volley of gunshots. She'd just about given up when she caught a flicker of red to her right. She zoomed in and almost crowed when the red shifted and moved. Too big and complex to be an animal.

Genevieve crawled out to the back room in the dark, trying her best not to make a single sound that would alert Alex, avoiding each of the creaky boards. He stirred once, when she opened the back door to allow the cooler air in, but he subsided back to sleep.

Alex's conclusion that the guy was playing with them was dead on. If she'd been in the shooter's place and wanted to get to someone who was inside this cabin? It would have been a simple matter to shoot out the sunroom. The whole wall and the back door were made of glass. Before she walked out the door, she did a quick survey of the forest from here. Once again, not foolproof, but it was all she had. If there was more than one aggressor, it made sense to have one of them parked out in the back.

She opened the door and crept out, flattening into the shadows of the house as soon as she was able. She held her breath, but no bullets came tearing out of the darkness toward her. When she was safe for a solid two minutes, she exhaled and started to inch toward the side she'd glimpsed the color from.

The snow crunched beneath her boots. Probably not that loud, but to her, it seemed like it was in stereo. Her gun was sweaty in her palms. She kept her vision off the physical plane in an effort to see any stray energy.

A plan that had seemed so simple inside now appeared fraught with danger. Had she really thought she could just shoot someone? Sure, she'd done a few things she wasn't proud of, but shooting someone with a gun was a hell of a lot more personal than cursing a person to a long and painful death.

By the time she reached the front corner of her cabin, she was tempted to march herself right back inside to the safety of her home and Alex's side. That was when she glimpsed the energy moving amongst the trees, closer now.

Trying not to let her stomach heave in fright, she bent down, picked up a large, snow-encrusted rock and threw it as far away as she could. Since she could hear the sound it made when it landed, presumably the shooter could too.

Sure enough, the energy became more visible as the person moved closer to the edge of the trees. She lifted her gun and sighted down the barrel.

His aura was disgusting, a combination of black and red. She felt like she was staring at putrid flesh and rotting maggots. Genevieve shook her head until her vision cleared, fighting the urge to gag. This man was...horrible. She'd never realized anyone could look like that. There was no redeeming quality in him.

You could just play around with those colors a little. Really punish him for everything he's done. Come on, he deserves it. Genevieve tried to focus past the seductive voice. No. She wasn't going down that road again. If at all possible, she wanted to come out of this alive, which meant she was going to rely on good, old-fashioned bullets.

Hands suddenly steady, she took aim. Her finger tightened on the trigger.

It wasn't much different from shooting at targets on a post, she thought dispassionately, as the energy flinched and flickered. She watched him tumble out of the forest. She made the decision in an instant, changing her aim. She shot again. The gunshots were muted, but everything after them, the thud of the man, Alex's yell from inside the cabin, sounded unnaturally loud.

Her vision flipped so everything appeared normal, including the dark form on the ground. Not really sure what she was doing, she started walking to where the man had fallen. When she was within a foot or two of his body, she heard her name called out. She didn't bother to turn around.

She knelt beside the stranger and touched his face. His eyelids flickered open. Both of her shots had hit her target, and she didn't need to examine him to ascertain he didn't have long to live. His gun had fallen out of his outstretched hand, and she kicked it aside. Blood was pouring from both injuries, turning the snow beneath him to a sickly pink. Ignoring his wounds, she patted him down, removed another small gun and a knife, and sent them the same way.

"Genevieve!"

She jumped when Alex grabbed her arm from behind. "What the hell have you done?"

She blinked at him over her shoulder. "I took care of things."

He looked down at the man and froze. She wasn't so far gone that she didn't see the recognition in his face. "You know him?"

"Paul Leonie." He spat the name out. "His brother killed my partner. I testified against him."

The man glared and coughed. "Told you...gonna kill you. Saw you fucking this chick, knew I could really make you suffer."

Genevieve shuddered. If she was a little less frozen, she might feel horror that this man had caught their most intimate moments. "So that's why he shot at you and then followed you up here? Vengeance?" Silly rabbit. She could have told him vengeance didn't work.

"Must be. Genevieve, come on, inside. Leave him. We don't know who's with him."

With the way Alex was scanning the darkness, his handgun

cocked and ready to fire, she realized he was expecting trouble. The layer of calm surrounding her allowed her to look down at the dying man. His eyes were open lasers of hate directed straight toward Alex. "You know, I can help you." The man's black eyes turned to her.

"Angel, inside…"

She grabbed the man's hair and tipped his head back to make sure he was listening to her. "I can help you, but I want you tell me if you have any other friends or accomplices out there."

"Genevieve—"

She didn't pay any attention, but watched the man's aura.

"No," he whispered.

Satisfied, she let him fall back on the ground. "He's by himself. I've already taken all of his weapons off him. Help me get him to the shed over there." Like hell she was letting him in the house or the barn. The shed was old, but it was solid and she had a padlock she could put on it.

"I'm not taking the man's word for it."

She looked up at Alex. "I can tell when a person's lying. He's not. Besides, if someone else was out here, we'd be dead by now."

Genevieve loved that he didn't ask her any further questions. He simply took her claim at face value, handed her his gun and bent down to haul the slighter man into a fireman's carry. At the movement, Leonie slumped forward, unconscious. "Show me where."

She pointed to the shed and then followed after she had gathered up the guy's weapons and tucked them into her coat. Soon Alex was lowering Leonie to the dirty floor. "I don't know how long he's going to last. He seems to be bleeding an awful lot."

Alex didn't sound as if he particularly cared, and Genevieve supposed she couldn't really blame him. The guy had shot Alex and left him for dead, but for the grace of God. Plus, after the terror of the last day and night, she wasn't too thrilled with Leonie either. He was an evil little man who had probably never done a lick of good in his life. Telling them no one else was in the woods was probably the first words of truth he'd uttered in a long time.

But you can't let him die.

She shut her eyes, trying to block out the insistent whisper that was attempting to penetrate her frozen calm.

He deserved it. Given half a chance, he would have had no compunction about killing both her and Alex.

You're not a killer.

She inhaled so hard, tears sprang to her eyes. No. Oh, God, no, she wasn't a killer.

Ignoring Alex's start of surprise, she rushed over to the man and knelt next to him.

"Genevieve, what are you doing?"

"I have to heal him."

"What are you talking about?"

She looked at him, so tall and strong. A burst of relief coursed through her. She wasn't a killer. She still didn't deserve him, but no matter what she'd done, no matter how much she regretted it...she had a choice here. She didn't have to take this one on herself. "I can't have a third death on my conscience. Let me do this."

To his credit, Alex didn't even blink at her words. Though he looked none too pleased at the idea of her touching the other man, he nodded and subsided.

She didn't bother to fix the man on the aural plane, since she feared it would be far too tempting to lose her head and wreak a little bit of havoc. Instead, she did what she'd done for Alex. Of course, this man wouldn't have the warmth, shelter and proper cleanliness she'd afforded Alex, but what the hell. He deserved to suffer.

By the time the wounds had sufficiently repaired, Genevieve and Leonie were both whimpering. Distantly, she heard Alex say something, his tone worried. The next thing she knew, he picked her up and was carrying her. "Padlock," she managed to croak. Though Leonie would be out for a while as he healed, there was no need to take any chances.

He hesitated, but sat her down outside the shed on the cold ground. Ice and snow froze her butt, but since the chill took her mind off the pain, she didn't mind. She heard the rattle of chains, and then he was carrying her again.

She felt the warmth as they entered the cabin, and he lowered her to the kitchen chair.

Something touched her lips, and she instinctively opened her mouth. The bitter liquid made her cough a little. Her emergency whiskey wasn't for the faint of heart. His worried face appeared in her line of sight. She wanted to ease the furrow between his brows. "Don't worry. Normal. Always a balance."

"Is this what happened after you fixed me?"

She inhaled, the pain already starting to recede. "Worse. You were in much worse shape."

"If I'd known..."

He didn't have to finish the thought. Genevieve knew he was wishing he'd tackled her before she healed the man. "Had to do it. You didn't freeze."

"Huh?"

"You must have come running when you heard the first shot. You didn't freeze."

Alex blinked. "I guess I didn't."

She could move now. She shifted her legs, conscious of the water pooling on the floor.

She noticed wetness dripping on her as well. Oh God, he was still shirtless and shoeless. Blood and water had left streaks across his chest. His skin had turned from brown to blue. "You're going to get frostbite."

He looked down, as if just realizing he had been exposed to the elements for far too long. "We're both shaking. Come on, let's warm us up."

Alex gathered her in his arms and lifted her from the chair. She tried to make a token protest. "Your shoulder—"

"Is fine. Hush."

The shock and pain must have numbed her, because she couldn't even work up the energy to care. He set her on her feet. She blinked at the harsh fluorescent lights of the bathroom. He stripped off his pants and boxers, and she allowed him to remove her clothes as well, standing there like a doll.

He cranked the shower to the hottest level. His lips were as blue as his skin, and she felt a spurt of real alarm and an impetus to move out of her daze. "Hurry, get in there."

He hauled her in with him, his body flinching at the first touch of warmth on his skin. Though he needed the heat more than her, he made sure the water fell over both of them. He picked up the bar of soap. "Stand still."

She obeyed as he washed her clean. He spent an inordinate amount of time scrubbing her hands and arms. To offer comfort, she figured, more than actually cleaning her. Since it kept him firmly under the hot spray as well, she didn't object.

Finally, Alex must have judged her to be clean or warm enough, since he shut the water off and reached out of the stall to grab the towel. He rubbed her down thoroughly before swiping at his own wet chest and tucking the towel around his waist. He used a dry towel to wrap her up, and then herded her from the bathroom. "Alex..."

"Hush."

She followed him into the main room and stood awkwardly, a stranger in her own home, while he locked the back door, checked the locks on the front and started a fire. The sudden light, after they'd spent a whole evening in darkness, seemed wrong in the room, and she cast a nervous glance at the window.

He noticed. "You're sure he was alone?"

"If there is someone else out there, he doesn't know about it. Did you check the phone?"

"When I got you the whiskey. Still dead." Finished with the fire, he stood and pulled the blanket off the bed before he walked toward her with a determined glint. "Drop the towel. I want to get you warm."

Uncaring of her modesty, she tossed the towel aside. The chill touched her for an instant before he wrapped the extra blanket around her. As if she weighed nothing, he picked her up in his arms again and sat down with her in the armchair. She didn't protest, only snuggled closer. "I can't seem to stop shaking. It's not because I'm cold, I think."

"Have you ever fired a gun at another person?"

"No."

"First time I had to fire a gun, you'd have thought I had palsy. It's a natural reaction. I'd be amazed if you could just laugh it off."

"I can't believe I shot a man." How could she have thought she could just kill a man and walk away?

"We're in perfect agreement, then. I can't believe it either. In fact, I can't believe you left me sleeping here and waltzed out there all by yourself with one measly shotgun against God knew how many bad guys."

His arms had grown tighter around her with every word he spoke. He hadn't raised his voice, but it didn't take a rocket scientist to figure out he wasn't too happy. She kept her tone mild. "I know it wasn't the smartest move. It seemed like a good idea at the time. I figured I could track the person by their energy and take them out that way. Otherwise, we were just sitting targets, Alex. We had to do something."

"And you couldn't include me in your plan, why?"

"Be honest. Would you have let me go out there, even if you were with me?" He didn't speak. "See? I had to do something. I couldn't stand the thought that someone was playing with us like that." She couldn't stand the thought of him getting hurt.

"I thought it was because of what I told you. I thought you figured I was useless."

Her heart caught at the naked shame in his voice. "Because of your PTSD? No! That wasn't the reason at all." She hesitated. "I admit, I did have some half-baked idea that I'd be able to better handle violence than you, but..." She wrinkled her nose. "Since you were the one who was willing to leave the guy to bleed out, and I had to go and get all girlie on you and help the villain, I guess that isn't the case."

"You do realize I worked narcotics in New York, don't you?" he asked, his tone dry. "Drug dealers don't settle their differences with a handshake and a cup of tea. I burned out because I lost someone I loved, not because I faint at the sight of blood."

She grinned, sheepish. "Yeah. I didn't really think of that. I think I went a little crazy when I saw your aura for the first time. That's all I can claim. It's so pure, and I figured since I was already...tarnished, I should be the one to do the deed."

"I don't understand this aura business very well, but I can tell you that I'm not a particularly pure or blameless person." When he turned his head to face her, Genevieve recoiled from the stranger facing her. Alex's expression was unemotional and flat. "I really don't care if Leonie dies. The only reason I let you heal him was because you seemed to need it. I wanted him to die when he was out there terrorizing us. The fact that he watched us making love..." Alex's jaw clenched. "I want him to burn in hell for that."

A full body shiver ran though her. Frankly, she was a bit freaked out by this side of her sweet, happy-go-lucky lover. "Um, yes, well. I figured out fast I'm a pretty weak assassin. Next time, you totally get to play the hero." Her lips twisted. "I...I figured I was so beyond redemption it didn't even matter."

"Why would you think that?"

She looked down at her hands. "You know how I said I couldn't have a third death on my conscience?"

"Yeah, that was interesting. Tell me about that."

Her mouth felt like the filter had been removed. She had no choice but to tell him, to make him understand. "Three years ago, I came home for a surprise visit. Two police cruisers were parked out front."

Alex's arms tensed around her, as if he could sense what was coming and wanted to stop it.

"I slipped around from out back. Your predecessor and two of his deputies were just leaving. They didn't see me and I heard one of the deputies ask what would happen if the witch told she'd been raped. Bainsworth said no one would believe her anyway, and they were the law, so who cared. The other man was mad and said that he didn't get a turn before she passed out. The chief clapped him on the back and said there was always next time." She faltered and he exhaled.

"I was so angry. It wasn't fair, and I didn't know how long it had been going on, and Mom had never said anything. To think of them raping her, when she was such a sweet, gentle woman, it made me so furious I couldn't think. And I knew they were right, that they were protected, that nothing would happen to them and I..." She took a deep breath. "When they saw me, the deputies got scared, but Bainsworth didn't seem to care. He laughed and started walking toward me, and I just..."

"What?" he prompted her when she faltered.

She turned stricken eyes on him. "I killed him."

Alex's tone was soft and reasonable. "He died seven months ago."

"Because of me. I wanted to give him the most lingering, dignity-sucking death I could imagine." She closed her eyes. "Do you understand? I gave him that tumor."

His hands stopped caressing her back. She waited for his skepticism, or worse, his disgust. She tried to fill the silence. "I can't just see auras; I can manipulate them on some level. Usually if someone's injured, I can tweak the colors to aid in healing. I had never done the opposite before in my life, but looking at his smug face, this little switch in my mind tripped and I knew I held his life in my hand. I'd never felt so powerful, so drunk with power. I could see his aura and I could see exactly what I needed to manipulate to make him sick.

"He staggered back and his deputies caught him. They all looked so scared of little old me. I loved it. I was so excited, I didn't even see my mother until she started screaming. I don't even remember what she said to them, but they beat tracks out of there. Mom came up to me, still screaming, and slapped me. She'd never hit me before in my life. She grabbed my hand, and that's the last thing I remember until I woke up a few hours later."

Genevieve shuddered. "It was dark inside the cabin. Mom sat in the rocking chair, and I was lying on the bed. I felt terrible, but I was more concerned with the way she looked. Her face was bruised and bloody. I tried to get her to go to the hospital, but she wouldn't listen, she just kept saying it was all too late."

"Too late for what?"

"The balance. There's always a balance. If I heal someone, I get hurt, at least for a little while. What they feel, times three. But I didn't feel sick, so it took me a bit to figure out what she'd done. After that night, it was like everything I had inside of me had been burned away. I spent my entire life wanting to be normal, but when my power was gone...I felt empty.

"Mom got sick, real fast. I don't know how she did it, but she took the rebound away from me and made it her own. Maybe that's why I lost my abilities. I couldn't heal her, I couldn't help her. All I could do was watch while she died a little every day for two years, while the tumor in her ovaries spread through her entire body. So because I couldn't control my anger, I killed my mother.

"She wasn't a normal woman. She was simple, she hated being around other people. I should have stayed. I owed her. She didn't just home-school me because she felt like it. It took her years to teach me to control my powers. I repaid her by leaving her here at the mercy of whoever happened to come along."

"That's quite the hair shirt you've been wearing there. It was tragic, yes, but I'd say a lot of that blame goes on those

three grown men, not a young woman. What were their names?"
His tone was very mild.

"Who?"

"You said Bainsworth was there with two other cops. Who
were the deputies?"

She paused. "Carlyle was one. I heard that he died a couple
years back in a car accident. I swear, I didn't have anything to
do with that," she added hurriedly.

He squeezed her. "And the other?"

"Reynolds."

"I always knew that guy was a little prick," he growled. "But
I'm glad he's around so at least I can kill one of them myself."

She twisted her neck around until she could see his face,
surprised at the level of outrage there. "I don't want him killed.
He's left me alone."

"When I get back to town that little pissant is going to be
lucky if he walks away with the beating of his life. I'll have his
job and his pension before I'm done. To terrorize an innocent
woman and a child, turn your life upside down, completely
isolate you, and then hide behind the law..." He shook his head.

She stroked his hand. Somewhere, she was amused that
she was soothing him instead of the other way around. "You
don't have to do that for me. I've carved out a life for myself. The
rumors spread and everyone left me alone."

"I'd do it for anyone," he said gruffly. "That you're who you
are only makes me want to do it a little more violently. Besides,
this is no life, and you know it."

Out of nowhere, giant tears pooled out of her eyes. Alex had
a typical male reaction. "Hey now. Okay. I didn't mean to slam
your life."

"It's not that. You're right. I hate it here. I thought I

deserved it."

"I like that."

"What?"

"Thought. Past tense. You need to know you don't deserve it."

"My mother—"

"Would want this life for you?"

"It was *my* fault. If I had been here instead of off having fun in the first place, she would have been fine."

Alex sighed. "That's a lot of ifs. How 'bout this one? How do you know, if you hadn't hurt Bainsworth, that he and his men wouldn't have raped you? Killed both you and your mother?"

She opened her mouth to answer, but found herself stumped. That possibility had never crossed her mind.

"It was self-defense, honey. Your powers were the weapon you had, and you instinctively used them. Now, yeah, it sucks about your mother, but she was an adult. She made her choice." He hugged her tight. "And I completely understand why she did it. Did you ever think that she might have felt like I do tonight? I led that asshole to your doorstep. It was my fault that you had to go out there with a gun and make the decision to shoot another human being. When I was in that shower with you, all I could think about was how I wished I could take that experience away from you and make it my own. When you look at it that way, how can you fault her at all for trying to mitigate the results? Don't tell me you wouldn't do it for someone you lo—cared for."

Genevieve pretended not to notice his slip. She made a fist and pressed it against her chest. "I still feel dirty. Logically, I know I'm not a killer." She shuddered. "Tonight proves that. It's hard to get past that sense of responsibility, though."

Gentle teasing lined his face. "My mama's a devout Catholic. I think you could give her lessons in guilt. I know you expect me to be disgusted or scared, but all I can feel is a bit of irritation that this was the big secret you've been hiding."

Though she knew he was looking to get a rise out of her, she couldn't help but bristle. "Being able to kill people with your thoughts is a damn big secret."

He gave a shrug. "I guess. Here I thought you were going to tell me you used to be a man or something. That would have been something to get all emo over."

She sniffed loudly. "Wow. Thanks."

Alex laughed and enfolded her in his arms. She closed her eyes and snuggled closer. Nothing had ever felt so good in her life.

He unclenched her hand from where it rested against her heart. "You're not dirty, or tarnished, or condemned, or anything else you want to call it."

"You can't see my aura."

"You're right. You know what, though? Us normal folk, we have to rely on things that aren't magical sometimes. My parents always taught me to judge people on their actions. And every action I've seen from you so far has proven to me that you're an amazing person who's had a couple of tough breaks."

"Once you go back to town and get away from these extraordinary circumstances—"

"I'll still think you're the most amazing woman I've ever met."

She stared at him, frustration and hope warring inside of her. "You just wait and see."

"Why don't we do that? A relationship between us isn't impossible. You could come with me. Or not," he added quickly when she tensed. "We could date, commute. Not everyone is like Bainsworth, Genevieve. I'm sure there are other people who care about you, like that grocer. And there's no rule that says you have to give up everything and conform to my life. We can live anywhere in the world. Or I could come out here."

Genevieve grinned. "Alex, I don't think you'd do well as a hermit. You're the type who needs people all around you. And I—I don't know if I'm ready to leave here yet."

He ignored the latter part of that statement. "Angel, I'd give up everyone in that town for you. I've never felt like this about another woman, like I'm in too deep to ever find my way out— and I'm willing to bet money you feel the same way." She opened her mouth to protest, but he hugged her tighter. "Answer me this: would you really have had sex with any man who ended up on your floor?"

"No. My body's pretty much been in deep freeze since the incident."

The instant response warmed his heart. He licked the shell of her ear. "I'm not playing with you. This is serious. We'll take it slow. Just don't shut me out again. Take some time to think about it."

Her eyes held fear and longing. "I'll think about it."

That was the most he could hope for. He kissed her, unable to continue holding her without loving her. Genevieve turned her head to the side and to keep her from arguing just for the hell of it, Alex latched on to her ear, nibbling it just the way he knew she liked. "I want to make love to you, but I don't want to be otherwise occupied if we have any more uninvited guests."

Her hand stroked over his neck, but she might as well have squeezed his cock. "That guy's gonna be out for a while."

Reluctantly, he disengaged. "Still. Why don't we take a break from sex until all of the bad guys have been carted off?"

Her brow furrowed in disappointment, but she nodded. He pressed her head against his chest. "Sleep."

Alex held Genevieve until his arms fell asleep. Then he picked her up carefully and laid her out on the mattress.

She was in a deep sleep, but nonetheless, he tried to be as quiet as possible as he went into the back room. He hated to leave her for even a minute. He wanted to stand guard over her sleeping body with a machine gun.

However, he needed clothes, and he hoped he'd find more garments in the storage closet he'd looked through earlier. He didn't want to put on anything that had come into contact with Leonie. That rat bastard. Genevieve wanted to talk about guilt? He was going to have nightmares that she had marched right out in the dark to confront a man he'd led to her doorstep.

He winced a bit to think of what his old buddies on the force would say if they knew a woman had taken the initiative because she'd thought his soul too pure to shoot another person. Alex's mouth firmed.

Nobody would know Genevieve had been the one to shoot Leonie. He'd make sure of it. Not for his ego, he was damn proud of her, but because he wouldn't have even a shadow of that ugliness touch her. It was what he deserved for sleeping through this. He hadn't been able to save his partner; he hadn't been able to protect Genevieve. At the very least, he could do this much for her, even if he had to gag or threaten her into sticking with his version of events. Since Leonie would probably survive the night—and wasn't that a shame—he'd rather be the target of any more vengeance schemes.

Alex rifled through the boxes, finding nothing but women's clothing. He shoved the boxes back in and started to go through the containers on the top shelf. Genevieve had suffered enough at the hands of other people in her life. She didn't deserve any more hurt.

Alex felt the tide of rage rising again, thinking of his predecessors actions. Someone must have known what the previous chief and his cronies were up to, and he was sure rape was just one of the sins to be laid at the man's feet. For sure, he'd be rattling some cages when he got back to town. And God help the people who had participated, however indirectly, in hurting his Genevieve.

He wanted to dig the man up and kill him again. Genevieve had seemed to think he would be disgusted by what she had done. Wrong. He held no illusions about small-town politics, and the truth was Bainsworth may never have served time for his crime. Plus, Alex's blood chilled to think of what three men could have done to her tiny body when she came across them had she not had a bit of magic up her sleeve. If she'd had a gun or a taser, he wouldn't have faulted her for shooting the three men. The only thing that sucked was that it had taken her mother away from her. Whatever deity or council had given the Boden women their power sure had a bastard of a safety clause on how they could use it.

Finally, Alex found another pair of sweatpants and a T-shirt that he might have a chance in hell of squeezing into. Wearing clothes after this week might take some getting used to, he thought with humor. Hell, he could probably be back in his jeans as early as...tomorrow. Once morning broke, he'd see if he could track down Leonie's vehicle. He'd quickly patted the guy down after Genevieve had done her magic with him, but no keys had been in his pockets.

He backtracked to the main room, shutting and locking the door behind him. Where before the thought of leaving Genevieve had made him extremely melancholy, he wasn't that sad anymore. Sure, she hadn't given him a concrete commitment, but they'd made progress this evening.

He sat next to front door, the handgun gripped firmly in his hand. Not the semi-automatic he'd hoped for, but it would have to do. Now that he knew he wouldn't freeze where Genevieve's safety was concerned...well, anyone who tried to hurt her wouldn't last long.

Chapter Thirteen

"Talking to you is exhausting."

"Maybe in a few years it won't be so bad." He studied her with a devilish glint in his eyes and stroked a hand over her leg where it rested on his stomach.

She was fully aware he was goading her, but she was too wrung out to rise to outrage. "I swear, you would argue with a post until it came around to your way of thinking."

"That's what my mom says. You're going to love her."

She rolled her eyes. She'd slept for about an hour, and then they'd spent the next couple of hours talking and teasing in bed, resisting getting up and facing reality. If she didn't know they had a killer locked up in her old shed, they would have looked like any other normal couple. A feeling that Alex was encouraging, in his suddenly relentless campaign to have her agree to a long-term relationship.

It was looking more and more attractive, no doubt about that. If it weren't for that insistent voice in her head screaming of responsibility and sacrifice, it would be a no-brainer.

A rumble of noise distracted both of them and a dimple popped into his cheek. "Hungry?"

Genevieve shrugged. "Guess so." She sat up and wrapped a sheet around herself. "Let me make something quick."

"I can help too."

"Great."

They set about pulling eggs and ham from her small fridge. Not ten minutes later, Genevieve discovered something new about herself.

She didn't like anyone in her kitchen.

"That pan isn't Teflon."

Alex looked up from the egg he was about to crack. "That's okay, I can just scrape it off."

Genevieve stared at him. "Scraping ruins the pans."

"But if it isn't Teflon, why do you care?" He cracked the egg and dropped it in the pan, breaking the yolk. "Oops." He beamed at her. "Sorry, I know you wanted fried. I can eat this one scrambled. I'll have better luck with the next one."

"No, *I'll* have better luck with the next one. Go sit."

Alex seemed surprised. "But I'm a decent cook!"

"You said you were a terrible cook."

"Any idiot can make eggs."

"Your eggs are burning, smarty." She stifled a laugh when he swore and lifted the pan from the burner. Edging him aside, she took the abused breakfast away from him. "I'm an excellent cook, Alex, and if I had the choice, I'd rather eat food that's excellent. So go make us a little place on the ground where we can sit and eat. And cuddle." She tacked on the end of the sentence to motivate him and snatched the spatula away.

Alex reluctantly returned to the floor and made them a nest of pillows and blankets. While flipping the ham, she prevailed upon him to at least wrap a sheet around himself. Alex grudgingly complied, only when she claimed she would be too distracted to eat, which was half-true. To reward him, she did give him a quick cuddle before sitting down with him and the food.

"Next time, I'll cook for you."

Genevieve smiled and spread some egg yolk on her toast. The man couldn't resist his caretaking streak. "I don't mind you cooking as long as it's not in my kitchen. With my pans."

He pursed his lips. "Well, it'll probably be safer on your stomach if I order out. I guess I may have stretched the truth a little when I called myself a decent cook. I can do cereal and oatmeal okay, but my brother swears the mac and cheese I made for his birthday picnic made him sick for a week. I'll put the food on the plates for you, though. Or if you're good, I'll volunteer to be the plate." He bobbed his eyebrows comically.

She chuckled, feeling more lighthearted than she could remember. She tucked away the thought that this could be their last meal together here. In his company, the simple food tasted gourmet, and between the frequent kisses and caresses, it took a while to empty their plates. He started to help her when she picked up their dishes, but she brushed his hands away. "I'll just soak these and wash them later."

He relaxed, the happy light still in his eyes. "So I guess next time I'll be doing the dishes too."

Genevieve snorted. "Frankly, I don't mind if you do the dishes *every* time."

She realized what she had said when the silence stretched out. She looked over her shoulder. Alex studied her with a small, knowing smile.

"I didn't mean to imply...I mean, that we'd be together..."

"I know exactly what you meant, baby. No pressure, remember?"

She returned to her small sink, almost near tears at his gentle understanding. How easy it would be to fall into this routine, to imagine them together, eating meals and doing dishes. But how would she fit into his life when they were in his world?

She looked at the window, where dawn's light had seeped around the edges of the curtain. She needed some time to compose herself and come to grips with whatever this was between them. She walked over to her bureau, grabbed her clothes and dressed.

"Where are you going?" he asked, scowling as he sat up.

"I know it's weird, but most people wear clothes even if they're inside the house, Alex."

"If you lived with me, that would be the first rule to go."

She forced a smile. "But you're right, I'm going outside. It's morning. We should see about finding that car and getting that...you know, the man taken care of." Ugh, in all of the upheaval, she'd practically forgotten about the killer on her land. She was glad she didn't have to deal with his death, but man, she wanted him locked away and gone.

She grabbed her coat from the door. "I'm going to go feed Barney first. Poor guy's probably starving by now. Why don't you stay here?"

"What? No way. We stick together until the cops come collect Leonie and fully search the woods. I'm sorry, honey." He held up his hands, no doubt in response to the irritation on her face. She so was not used to someone telling her what to do. "Look, I think I've pretty much proven what an accommodating guy I am. Hell, I'm sure most people are going to call me henpecked. But when it comes to your continued good health, I'm afraid I'm going to be a bit of an ass. You might be a crack shot, but you aren't going out there again without me. Period."

Genevieve gave a gusty sigh. The obstinate set of his jaw told her this was one battle she wouldn't be winning. "Fine."

He dressed in another ancient pair of sweatpants and a ragged T-shirt he must have discovered in her storage closet. Despite the ridiculousness of the outfit, Genevieve felt a pang of sadness. She'd gotten used to her naked hunk wandering around, or when he was in the sheet, her gentle gladiator. Genevieve shook off the poetic thought. "You can't walk around in the snow with no shoes."

"Way ahead of you." He picked up a huge pair of tattered sneakers next to the chair. "I don't know why you had these in your home. They're too big for me, but I'll take them."

"I don't know either. My mom was a packrat. I'm impressed you found them. Now tell me you scrounged up a coat somewhere."

"Nope." He picked up her handgun, tucked it in the waistband of his sweatpants and wrapped a blanket around himself. "This'll have to do. I'm used to much colder weather. This is really nothing to me."

She grabbed her rifle and opened the door. The cold was nowhere near as freezing as it had been over the past couple of days. Good for the roads, bad for her heart. She tried to sound light. "Tough guy."

"I have to be, or you'll walk all over me."

They checked the shed first, Alex going in ahead of her with his gun cocked. Leonie was still out cold. The place was freezing, but when she mentioned that fact to Alex, he just gave her an incredulous look. "He's lucky he's alive and not in the snow. I'll be damned if I let you give him so much as a blanket."

She hid a smile. "I think you misinterpreted my tone. I didn't mean, 'Awww. His wittle toes must be cold!' I meant, 'Sweet, he must be cold.'"

"I'm glad to hear that. You had me wondering where my tough woman had gone to."

They continued to banter as they walked to the barn. He stopped as they reached the barn, his expression dissolving into bliss as he inhaled deeply of the smoke and apple scent in the air. He looked out into the distance and Genevieve followed his gaze, trying to see her home as he saw it, a dot of civilization wrestled from the tangled wilderness around it. Tall and mighty, the trees stood like sentinels guarding her little clearing—she knew each of them, had played within their shelter as they grew with her. The sun was just starting to rise above the horizon, splashing fingers of crimson and burnt umber over the woods, colors so bright they almost hurt the eye. "It's beautiful, Genevieve."

She nodded and swung open the door to her little ramshackle barn. "See? There are upsides to living here. That right there makes up for a lot of problems."

"I don't think I've ever seen a sunrise like that."

"Yeah, you can almost feel it, can't you?" Genevieve walked into the barn, sensing Alex behind her. "Come meet Barney," she said over her shoulder. The old horse, hearing his name and her voice, poked his brown head over the stall door, ears pricked.

"Uh, I can just wait here while you do...whatever you need to do."

She turned to look at him standing just inside the barn door. "Don't tell me you're scared of my old horse?"

He fidgeted and then scowled. "Of course not. I'm just enough of a city boy to appreciate that you shouldn't be too close to something that could crush you just by lifting a foot."

Genevieve laughed and entered the stall. Barney nudged her and then tossed his head in displeasure. "I'm sorry, baby. That man outside has me so turned inside out I forgot to bring you a treat. Next time, okay?"

Barney whinnied. She buried her face in his soft brown coat and gave him a hug to make up for her forgetfulness before starting to clean up, humming under her breath.

Had Barney not been so quiet, she would have missed the thud from outside the stall. She frowned and looked up. "Alex?" she called out. "Did you knock something over?"

Almost as an afterthought, she grabbed the rifle propped against the stall door before she walked out, the remnants of sun sending rays of light through the many cracks and holes in the barn's roof. A crimson shaft haloed Alex where he sprawled on the ground, mixing with the blood pooling under his head.

For a second, she felt her head spin with déjà vu. "Alex?" she whispered.

"Well now, sugar, this is quite a surprise."

Chapter Fourteen

Adrenaline mingled with shock as their intruder stepped out from the shadows to her left. It had been over four years since Genevieve had last seen him, and time had not been kind to Deputy Tom Reynolds. His face was bloated and red, his body soft and straining at the seams of his dirty and torn uniform.

She had been prepared for eventually confronting the man and dealing with her demons, but she wasn't ready for the ugly-looking gun he pointed at her chest.

"Drop the gun."

She wasn't about to argue, and she tossed it to the ground. She looked in Alex's direction, frantic at his stillness and the amount of blood under his head. Under the blanket, she couldn't even tell if he was breathing.

Reynolds licked his fat lips, making them shiny and wet. "You're all grown up now, aren't you, girl?" he whispered hoarsely. She could see the perverted lust in the beady eyes that roved over her body. He gave an ugly sneer. "I should have had you a long time ago, witch. Would have, too, if Bainsworth hadn't gone all crazy and threatened to shoot my dick off if I came out here. It's like God's looking out for me now, though. You and this bastard"—he spit at Alex's body—"all at the same time, like a nice little present. Yessiree, it's certainly fated."

Genevieve struggled to keep her calm while her mind raced. The deputy might be older, but he held the gun competently on both of them, his attention split equally.

Okay, Alex. Your turn to be the hero. I'll just stall him. Please wake up. "Why did you hurt him? What are you doing here now?"

He shrugged, the look in his eyes not quite sane. "I was supposed to get Bainsworth's job. He promised me. Kept waiting and waiting for it, and the power. And then that goddamned council had the nerve to pass me over for some goddamned outsider." He snickered. "But I took good care of that prick, yes, I did."

Genevieve swallowed. "Alex? Were you the one who shot him?"

Confusion clouded his gaze. "He was supposed to be dead. I thought I was so lucky when I saw him stop his car on that deserted stretch. I had already called the guy in New York, Leonie, to tell him I would help him kill the cop who put his brother away. But he hadn't showed up yet. Thought maybe I could get rid of Rivera, and maybe even get more money for killing him than I had got just for agreeing to work with the guy to trap him alone." Reynolds shook his head. "But I couldn't find his body and then Leonie showed up and yelled at me. Said he'd find him on his own. Said he wouldn't pay me nothing. I've been following him. Have you seen him?" he asked in the most polite tone, as if he were asking if she'd seen an old classmate.

Genevieve shook her head.

Reynolds mulled that over and shrugged. "Oh well. I'd rather have the job than the money. I need to take Rivera's body so the council will know he's dead. I'll say Leonie killed him, and they can make me chief." He stepped closer to her menacingly, the gun never wavering in his hand. "You're my perk." Reynolds gestured with the gun. "Let's go, you're coming with me."

"What?"

"Did you really think I would let you walk away? I've been ready to fuck you since you were twelve. We're gonna make sure this son of a bitch is good and dead and then I'll take you to my cabin by the lake and keep you there. Who's gonna report you missing?" His high-pitched giggle emerged again.

She lifted her chin, despite the ice-cold fear in her veins. "You do remember what happened to Bainsworth and Carlyle, don't you?"

"Those idiots weren't really cursed. It was just a coincidence." Yet Genevieve spotted a hint of uncertainty in his eyes that she capitalized on ruthlessly.

"Are you sure you want to risk that? Are you willing to bet your life on it?"

Reynolds was sweating now. "You're lying."

Genevieve shook her head with mock regret. "You know, this negative energy amplifies my powers," she bluffed. "You'd best leave now while you're still safe."

For a second, she thought maybe he'd actually do it, just walk away. Instead, his lips firmed, and he took a step toward her.

She felt a sinking sensation in her stomach. Though Reynolds was older, he was still a huge man. She would be no match for him physically.

Her eyes shot to Alex. She almost whooped with glee when she realized his right hand no longer lay on the floor by his head; it had disappeared under the blanket. Oh God, oh God, the man was awake. Bless his heart.

She looked back at Reynolds and tried not to give her

excitement away. The deputy was still too close to Alex, and he had both of them in his sights. She had to work out some sort of distraction. She had no idea what, if anything, Alex had planned, but he'd had a gun on him, and anyway, wasn't the damsel in distress's best option always a distraction?

Without another second of consideration, she concentrated until Reynolds's body no longer existed as flesh and blood, but as a miasma of colors. Brushing past the layers she didn't care for, she found the one she sought and attacked the weakest part of it.

Reynolds's brow furrowed. "What are you doing?"

She remained silent as he coughed.

"Stop it, bitch," he gasped. The aura flared a dark, pulsing purple. Not the gentle color of healing, but the rich, complicated hue of death. Part of her brain acknowledged the way his eyes bulged in panic.

The power; God, the power was so heady. It sucked on her, the seductive call of destruction.

Stop it. Stop it. Going too far.

Can't.

Her consciousness struggled against the excitement of knowing she had her enemy in her grasp, hers to do with whatever she pleased.

Alex.

The darkness within her receded at the thought of him, and she grasped on to it like a lifeline. She couldn't get sucked in here. Alex would be devastated if she succumbed.

The sharp crack of a gun brought her out of her spell, and she instinctively dropped to the floor.

She lay on the ground, trying to figure out where she had been shot.

And then she realized that other than the dull pain on her hip where she had landed, she felt remarkably healthy.

A loud groan prompted her to open her eyes a crack.

"Angel? Genevieve, are you okay?"

Reynolds lay in a heap on the concrete floor, blood seeping out from under his fingers where they clutched his shoulder. Alex stood some feet away from her, his face ashen, blood trickling from his head, and holding her handgun. He walked to her, stooping along the way to scoop up the deputy's fallen weapon.

He grasped her arms. "Did he hurt you?"

She shook her head. "No. Oh, Alex, he was the one who shot you."

"I heard. I knew he was a little bastard, but who knew so many people wanted me dead?"

Assured of her safety, he turned back to the fallen man. "Can you fetch me some rope, sweetheart?"

She scurried to the tack room, bringing back coils of heavy rope. She stopped when she realized that the deputy was unconscious, and there was a hell of a lot of blood covering his face that hadn't existed before she'd left the room. Alex stood over him with a very bland expression. "He was resisting arrest."

"Um, sure."

Alex grinned and made quick work of hog-tying the man, wrenching harder than necessary on his arms. When he had tied him to his satisfaction, he patted him down, removing two knives and some crushed mints. "Damn it, why is no one carrying car keys in their pockets?"

"Maybe he rode a horse."

"Can you honestly see this ass on a horse?" Alex stood and

endured Genevieve's fussing over his head with a stoic expression. "It's not that bad. You know how head wounds bleed. I'm almost ashamed he got the drop on me."

Genevieve snorted and rested her fingertips against his injured temple. "Yeah, when I get smacked in the head, my first emotion is shame too. Hold still." She concentrated. He held completely rigid, though she noticed his eyes flick upwards when her fingers started to glow purple. After a few minutes, she released him and transferred her hand to her own temple and rubbed. "Whew. I think I need some sugar. I'm getting too old for this stuff."

Alex reached up and tentatively felt the wound, which had stopped bleeding and subsided to an angry red bump. "You're amazing. Like my own walking Tylenol. You okay?"

She dropped her hand. "Yeah. It takes a bit out of you is all."

Alex pressed a kiss against her forehead, a tender motion. He drew back and eyed her in admiration. "By the way, thanks."

"For what?"

"For letting me feel like a man and save you for once."

"Oh. Yeah, I was hoping you had something up your sleeve."

"Or tucked into my sweatpants, as it were."

"I saw you move your hand. I had complete trust in your ability to save us," she added, in case he might have some doubts on that front. It must be tough to reconcile a weakness with that natural machismo.

She thought maybe he stood a little taller. "Thanks. I was just waiting for the guy to get distracted."

She puffed out her chest. "You know, distractions are totally the heroine's job."

"That tops the list as one of the best ever acts. How did you make yourself glow purple on command like that?"

"Acts? Oh. It was, you know. Just something I can do." Genevieve glanced away, scuffed her toe along the ground.

"Oh hell, no."

"Hmm?"

"Please tell me that was just an act. Please tell me you weren't going to do to him what you did to Bainsworth."

"Of course not." She hadn't had any intention of giving the guy cancer. That would have taken too long.

"You were going to fucking kill him! I can't believe that, Genevieve."

Her skin turned icy cold. "I'm sorry. I was trying to help. I realize that seeing what I can do in action might be a bit distasteful to you..."

"You think I'm mad because you have the ability to kill him?" Genevieve had no idea Alex could look so outraged. "I'm pissed because, according to the fucked-up rules of your universe, you'd be sacrificing yourself if you hurt him. You said it was a distraction, but what if you hadn't been able to control it? You've been out of practice with your powers for a while. Jesus Christ, I can't believe you. Dear God, Genevieve, I don't ever want to see you in this kind of situation again."

Though he wasn't exactly in a sweet and cuddly mood, she couldn't resist giving him a hug. A protective male was so cute. "Well, to tell you the truth, I'm not too fond of it either."

Reynolds chose that moment to let out a low moan. They looked down to see him blinking up at them before rage contorted his features at the sight of Genevieve in Alex's arms. "You son of a bitch. You're supposed to be dead."

Alex snarled. He let go of Genevieve and reached down to

grab the man by his collar. Genevieve winced as he hauled back and threw a punch to the man's face that snapped his neck back. "That's for shooting me, asshole." He punched him twice more, until Reynolds lay limp again on the floor. "And that's for hurting my woman." He rose from his crouch and held out his hand to Genevieve. "Was that fucking pure?"

"Nope." No one but he would understand how happy that made her either. "That was awesome."

"Come on, angel. Let's take care of this piece of shit first." He led her out of the barn and frowned at the sky as she closed the doors and snapped the padlock for good measure. "I'm sure Reynolds must have driven here. You know this area—where would he have hidden his car?"

After some searching, they found the vehicle hidden behind some brush about a quarter mile out. Alex grinned at the sight of the car and practically rubbed his hands in glee. "It's his cruiser. We've got a radio. Time to call the cavalry in." He paused. "But first, let's get all of our stories straight."

Chapter Fifteen

"Did you just make the sign of the cross?"

Alex's aggrieved question, directed toward a wide-eyed deputy, would have made Genevieve smile if she wasn't feeling quite so miserable.

They had managed to call the cavalry in, or what passed for the cavalry in Harrison, a few old patrol cars and pretty much the entirety of the police force. The dispatcher had been shocked to hear Alex's voice, and even more stunned when he'd told her where he was. Apparently, after shooting Alex, Reynolds had moved his car to the lake, almost fifty miles away from where he'd actually been injured. The search party had been braving the blistering cold to search in absolutely the wrong place.

The target of Alex's ire was a young man Genevieve knew by sight as someone who'd been a couple of years behind her in school. He'd been an idiot back then. Nice to see things hadn't changed.

"N-n-no, sir."

Alex pinned him with a gaze so black, Genevieve was relieved that she wasn't on the receiving end of it. "Are you finished taking her statement?"

"Yes. I'll, uh, go see if they need any help with that guy." Genevieve guessed the guy was Leonie. Or maybe the deputy just wanted to be away from her.

Alex sighed and dropped to squat in front of her where she sat huddled on her porch steps. "Did you stick with our story?"

Genevieve knew the others were out of earshot, otherwise Alex wouldn't have risked asking. "Yes. I said you shot Leonie." Leonie's car had been found a little farther west than Reynolds'. Since it had been filled with all sorts of incriminating evidence, Genevieve wasn't too worried about Alex being formally charged, though she wasn't thrilled with his decision to absolve her of any blame. She had questioned what would happen when Leonie's wounds healed quicker than they otherwise should, but Alex had shrugged and said people would just consider it a miracle.

"And you downplayed my injury?"

"I said when I found you, your greatest worry was a bullet crease and frostbite. Nothing a bandage and chicken soup wouldn't cure."

"Okay. Good." He stared at the ground between his feet. "You weren't kidding, were you?"

"That everyone in that little town hates me? No sirree, Bob."

He looked up and smiled. "And here I thought the biggest stumbling block would be people who frowned on an interracial relationship."

"I wish." She cast an uneasy glance at where the pack of police officers stood huddled together. She didn't like the way they were staring over at the two of them. "Alex, you need to go."

He reached out to touch her face, but checked his motion when she flinched back. His hurt expression tore at her heart.

She had to make him understand, and quickly. Whatever hope she'd had that they could ease into a relationship had been steadily demolished when the other people had intruded on their seclusion. "Listen up. This is the real world now. You think you're going to have a job or a place in that town if word gets back that you were sharing my bed? Be rational." His job meant so much to him. She'd caught that from him. The man didn't care how or where he did it, as long as he was a cop.

"I don't care what anyone thinks."

"Alex." She closed her eyes in an effort to compose herself. "I...I think I could love you very easily. But I can't just give up everything I've pledged myself to. I'm sorry." The words cost her. With him around, she'd started to really believe she didn't need to do penance for the rest of her life. Once he left, though, it would be tougher to rationalize.

He waited to speak until she opened her eyes. His expression was a mix of anger and resignation. "This isn't about being a part of the real world. We could work something out."

How could they? Still she knew if he was given half the chance, he would turn his life upside down for her. He was so damn noble. She had to be the one who was thinking with the brain instead of the heart. "Your mom and brother are waiting for you, aren't they?"

He frowned at the reminder and stood immediately. She would have felt guilty about knowing exactly what would worry him most if she wasn't so heartsick. "I'll come back..." he began, in a quiet tone.

She looked over at the knot of deputies, catching the same young guy making the sign to ward off evil. The little man paled when he noted her watching him. "No. Please. I don't want you to. There's no way it could ever work between us. I can't see you in that town without making myself miserable and you can't come here and still be happy." Sensing his wavering, she brought out the big guns, real tears welling in her eyes.

"Please...please don't hurt me more by coming back here and showing me what I can't have."

He opened his mouth, only to close it and swallow hard. When he spoke, his voice was hoarse. "No. No, I'll never hurt you." He stuck out his hand, and feeling a bit surreal, she grasped and shook it. "Thank you for everything. I'll...I'll never forget it."

He turned around, whistled to the other men. With varying degrees of speculation and looks of fear leveled at her, they climbed into their cars and started to make their way out of the snowy land.

Genevieve sat on her porch for a while after they left. It was cold and damp, the wet plank floor seeping into her jeans to freeze her butt, but she couldn't go inside and face the aching loneliness of her small cabin.

For the first time in three years, she understood an inkling of what her mother must have felt. Sacrificing to protect someone you loved from themselves hurt like hell.

But sometimes there just wasn't any other choice.

Chapter Sixteen

Three weeks later

"Folks, get your snow gear ready, 'cause we have a doozy of a storm heading our way—" The announcer's voice was cut off as Genevieve hit the dial on her brand-new HD radio. The thing had been dropped on her doorstep yesterday, the latest in a series of presents.

It joined the ranks of a state-of-the-art shortwave radio, a prepaid cell phone that received amazing coverage even out here, a case of ammunition, pristine pots and pans, a box full of gourmet canned foods, and—her favorite—a box of lacy lingerie, the exact same brand she'd loved to wear in her old life.

The gifts had started showing up in the middle of the night twenty-four hours after she'd sent Alex packing. She'd cried over the shortwave, the first one, knowing it was a gesture to show how concerned he was over her safety. Then, a few days later, she'd gone out in the morning to find the next one.

There was no rhyme or reason to how he was staggering them out, or what his point was. That he could make her life easier? Maybe. That he was up to the task of protecting her? Probably. That he was thinking of her? Absolutely.

And she couldn't stop thinking about him. Everything in her home screamed his name, from her bed to the shower to the kitchen. She couldn't get away from it. Nor did she really want to. She wanted him back. In her life. In her bed.

God, yes, in her bed. Who said love couldn't start from good old animal attraction? She stared into the fire and curled her legs deeper underneath her in the armchair.

The fact that he was coming so physically close to her to leave her the little presents was driving her crazy too. Though she might have to wait a while for another visit. The forecaster had confirmed what the little flurries she'd noticed while eating dinner had told her.

The thump on her porch had her heart jumping in her throat before she darted a glance at her wristwatch. It was dark, but barely nine. Besides, Alex had never made any noise before.

A bit nervous, she crossed to her bureau to remove her handgun before she walked to her window, twitched the curtain aside, hit the light and peered outside.

A box. A large brown box sat on her porch. And it was...moving?

Intrigued, she opened her door to hear a plaintive howl come from inside the thing.

She had her suspicions and they were confirmed when she opened the flaps to find a tiny golden puppy staring up at her and shivering. Mostly lab, she guessed, though there was definitely some pure mutt running through his veins.

The pup mewled again, and she couldn't take it. As she reached in to pick him up, he went into a frenzy of excitement, his small body wriggling, the heat of his heart warming her hands. She brought him up to stare into his deep eyes. The poor guy just about stroked out trying to reach her nose with his tongue. "A radio, I understand. What's your practical purpose?"

"He doesn't have one."

Even though she was half expecting it, she jumped as Alex stepped onto the porch. He looked tired and...hot. She realized she was seeing him fully dressed for the first time, and wasn't that a kicker? His jeans fit him perfectly, a battered leather jacket hiding the rest of him.

"I figured you had enough practical gifts. You needed something unpractical."

"Impractical."

His dimple, that beloved dimple, winked. "That too. Anyway, I couldn't come up with anything more impractical than that goofy mutt."

Without thinking, she brought the puppy closer to her chest. "He's not goofy. He's a baby." She jumped when the dog tried to burrow under her shirt.

Alex smiled. "He's cold. So am I. May we come in, Genevieve?"

He was so polite, it seemed weird. As if he was reading her thoughts, he raked his hands through his hair. "I didn't ask the first time. Figured you deserve a choice."

Though she was finding it a bit difficult to breathe, she nodded. After collecting the dog bowl in the box, she held the door open for him. When he came inside, she noticed that he was holding two duffels.

He raised the smaller one. "This is everything you'll need for the dog. If you want to keep him. If not, I'll take him back."

She looked down at the guy, cradled like a baby in her arms. He watched her with complete trust and blind adoration already and gave a tiny bark. "I'll keep him."

To give herself something to do, she filled up the bowl with water and set it down. When she deposited the dog on the ground, he gave a growl and attacked the bowl as if it were his enemy.

They laughed at his antics, and it seemed to break the tension and weird formality of the moment. When she looked at him, he was smiling, a sheen of moisture in his eyes. "Reynolds and Leonie are both behind bars. Leonie didn't get bail, and Reynolds's is too high. He seems to have lost all of his friends."

Satisfaction flowed through her. "Good. I hope Reynolds is finding out what they do to cops behind bars."

"I'm sure he has. I've missed you."

"Me too." She couldn't help the admission. She cleared her throat. "So what is the deal with the presents?"

The tips of his ears turned pink. "I was courting you."

"With radios and canned food?"

"I figured you'd appreciate that more than flowers and candy."

She smiled. He had her pegged. "And the lingerie?"

"Well, yeah, so not everything was practical. But everyone needs panties, right?"

"The thong isn't considered a necessity."

His eyes flared with heat. "Depends how you're looking at it."

Her breath caught. Forget how good his rangy body looked in clothes, she wanted to do nothing more than tear them off. Her brain taunted her with how good he'd looked lying on her bed in nothing but a sheet.

"Anyway, the weather kind of derailed my plan. I couldn't stand the thought of you spending another snowstorm here by yourself. So..." He lifted the larger bag.

"So you're planning on getting snowbound with me?" She shook her head in disbelief. "Did you use your vacation days for

191

this?"

"Kind of. Every day's a vacation day for me. I quit my job."

"What?"

He dropped the duffel on the floor and shrugged out of his jacket. Underneath, the white long-sleeved shirt molded to his muscles and brought out the tan of his skin. "I handed in my resignation. I'm done."

"But...you can't do that. You love being a cop!"

"Yeah, but you made me realize something. I loved being a cop because I felt like I was making a difference in the world. I'm not doing jack shit here except sort paper."

"There's different levels of—"

"Genevieve, I get that. I have nothing but respect for small-town law enforcement. This timeout has been good for me. I needed it, but Harrison doesn't need me. When I handed in my resignation...I'm officially no longer a cop, and ask me how I feel."

"How do you feel?" she asked cautiously.

He grinned. "Like me. I thought I couldn't live without this job, without this title. But I don't need it. I'm still me. Thanks to you, I feel confident in a way I didn't before. I don't think I'm magically cured, but it's like a weight was lifted off me. Like I've been redeemed. I don't need to be a cop to feel like a hero, because when you look at me, I'm already there.

"When I came here, I was so desperate to find any way I could to remain a cop, even if I was unhappy doing it. If I get another job in law enforcement, it will be because I really want it and I'm able to handle it, not because I can't do something else."

She smiled back, thrilled for him. "That's great. I'm happy for you."

"So, you see, you don't need to stay away from me to protect my precious job. It's fine."

"That's not the only reason..."

"It was a big one. Admit it." When she hesitated, he pursued. "If you still can't leave here, Genevieve, I'll move in with you."

"You'd do that?"

Alex's face was very serious. "We all sacrifice stuff for the people we love, don't we?"

"You really love me?"

"I think I fell the second I opened my eyes on your porch. One way or another, Genevieve, we're going to end up together. Call it fate or magic, but I know we were meant to meet. It may not have been the most ordinary circumstances, but I know you better after this experience than I would have ever gotten to know you through a month of scheduled dates. Don't tell me you didn't feel something special the first moment you touched me. Tell me you didn't feel a spark when we kissed. Tell me the world didn't move when we made love."

"I can't tell you any of that." She looked up at him, certain her heart was shining in her eyes. "You want the truth? I have my own bag packed and ready to go. Once the storm cleared out, I was planning on hunting you down. Life's not much fun without you."

He looked a bit stunned. "You would have come to me, even though you thought I work in a town you despise?"

"Yeah, well. We all sacrifice for the ones we love, don't we?"

He stilled completely at the word love. Then his relieved grin just about split his face and he walked over to crush her in his arms. "Lucky for you, we don't have to. We can live here if you want. If you need to."

"I hate it here, and I know you wouldn't be able to stand the isolation." She turned her head so her voice wouldn't be muffled. "Life's too short to bring yourself misery. I don't know if I'll ever completely forgive myself for the part I played, but I keep replaying what you said, about how my mom didn't sacrifice herself only for me to throw my life away." It was time to grow up, and grasp the happiness he offered. She'd wasted years trying to atone for what she'd done, but she realized now how deeply upset her mother would have been if she knew how she'd been living. She'd been ready to sacrifice herself for Alex, not once, but twice. She could empathize with what her mother had done out of love for her. She'd do the same for her own child.

He nuzzled her hair. "I told you, there's nothing for you to feel guilty—"

She brushed a light kiss against his jaw, and he shuddered. Against her stomach, his cock hardened and lengthened beneath the denim of his pants. She really did resent his clothes. Genevieve slowly stroked his pecs, loving the feel of him, now familiar but no less exciting.

Alex was a risk, yes, but it could have huge payoffs. She started to unbutton his shirt. "So we're both technically unemployed and don't know where we'll live. How does that sound to you?"

"If you're in the equation? Perfect." Alex smiled. She glimpsed happiness and relief in his eyes before his head swooped down on her lips. "You won't regret it. I'm going to keep you too satisfied to regret it," he promised her as he stripped her shirt off with such force she heard buttons snapping. He lowered his head, pushing her breasts together and burying his face between them. He licked and sucked, causing her to moan loudly.

"Alex, let's get in bed."

His mouth drove her crazy, working her nipple through her bra. "We can finish in the bed. We'll start here."

He fell to his knees and grabbed the waistband of her loose jeans, pulling them and her panties down with a quick tug. He nibbled and licked the insides of her thighs.

Just that easily, her body was ready for his. "Take off your clothes too."

"Whatever you want." He stood with a rakish grin and yanked off his shirt, unbuttoned and unzipped his jeans, dropping them to his feet along with his boxers and standing before her wonderfully nude. Ahhh, yes. She might insist he stay naked for the rest of their lives.

She took a second to rest a hand over his unscarred shoulder, where his wound had once marred the flesh. He looked down and covered her hand. The silence between them was full of unspoken gratitude and relief. He rubbed his thumb over her hand, the stroke bringing her back to the here and now. She caught his gaze and tried to lighten the suddenly heavy mood. "I love it when you follow directions."

His smile widened. "I live to serve."

"Ooooh. I like the sound of that." She slapped a hand on his naked chest and walked them backwards until the back of his knees hit her bed. He sat down with a thump. "You know, in all the craziness we forgot all about those dominatrix fantasies of yours."

Alex snorted. "Let's be honest as to whose fantasies they are."

"You got me. Lie down."

His expression was full of condescending amusement as he lay back on her mattress. A rush of possessive need flowed through her at the sight of his hard brown body spread before her like her own personal banquet of sex.

"Put your arms above your head."

He obeyed, still wearing that irritating manly smirk. Her eyes narrowed. Did he honestly not comprehend her power yet?

She put a little extra sway into her hips as she turned away, and she knew his gaze was all over her. She opened her bureau drawer and found exactly what she needed.

Alex didn't think he'd ever been so happy in his life. His body was whole, he was in a warm place, the puppy had flopped down to sleep by the roaring fire, and he was with the woman he loved. Sure, their future was uncertain, and as she'd noted, they were both unemployed and essentially rootless, but he couldn't quite lose his optimism. They'd make it, one way or another.

He hadn't entirely planned on jumping into bed with her tonight. He'd had some vague idea of them having a very adult and mature conversation the whole night long. Unfortunately, she'd had to go and breathe. That was apparently all it took for him to lose all rational thought.

Her body was lit by the light of the fire and her reading lamp. Her plump thighs rubbed together when she walked away from him to her chest of drawers. He wished he could insert his cock between those legs, let that silk rub him to orgasm. He loved how completely at ease she'd become in being naked with him. He loved her basic sweetness, her gentleness, which she kept hidden under a prickly exterior. Loved...her.

His sweet, gentle woman turned to him.

With scarves in her hands.

"Stretch your arms above your head and don't move them. No matter what." A dimple winked. "Please." The request was actually more of an order and Alex balked.

"Um, angel..."

"Do it."

Aw, hell. His personality didn't really lend itself to abdicating control. But now that he thought about it, he wanted no doubts to linger between them that he had coerced her or taken advantage of her.

He extended his arms above his head. "Fine. You're in charge. Don't get too used to it. And no funny business."

Genevieve frowned. "It doesn't hurt, right? Stretching your arms like that?"

Like a complete sap, he melted to goo. "It's fine. Hasn't hurt for a while now."

She straddled his chest and tied his hands to the headboard with quick motions. He resisted the urge to strain against the bonds. Then she leaned in close, tracing a forefinger along his biceps. The muscles jumped in response to her touch.

"I think you're missing out if you institute a no-funny-business clause. I've read that some of that funny business can be quite pleasurable."

Alex shivered at her breath on his neck. "I want some guidelines. Number one, my ass is my own, angel."

Her pert nose wrinkled and she sat back on his stomach. He could feel the curls on her sex getting progressively wetter, could smell her arousal, which had his cock rising in appreciation behind her. "Yeah, you can keep your ass. I never understood the attraction of that whole deal anyway."

A violent possessiveness rose within his chest. He had never gone for anal sex much either, but instinct urged him to brand himself on every part of her body he could reach. "Let me tie you down later," he rasped. "And we can explore it."

She rolled her eyes. "Whatever."

"Number two..."

"Bored now." Before he could even guess as to her intent, she leaned down and bit gently at his right nipple, then laved it with her tongue. He subsided with a groan and relaxed against the fresh sheets. So he would give up a little bit of control. It wouldn't kill him. Except maybe with pleasure. Her silken body slowly moved down his, her hair tickling his abdomen. He grunted when his cock brushed through the warm valley of her breasts. Her gaze darted up to him, violet sparks flashing in her exotic eyes. "You like that?" She deliberately rubbed her body against him again.

"Oh, Jesus, yes."

She pleasured him for a minute before he gathered his energy to speak. "Use your hands. Wrap yourself around me."

She moved away from him without warning, and he opened his eyes in shocked hunger. Her stubborn chin tilted up. "Maybe we do need a few more rules. For the next little while, I'm in charge. You don't give any orders."

He laughed before he realized she was completely serious. "Or what?"

"Or..." she leaned down and swiped her tongue over the head of his sensitive cock, "...I'm going to gag you. Do we need to do that right now?"

"I think I can manage," he gasped. Alex would have agreed to anything, just to feel that tantalizing flesh all around him again.

"Good boy." She teased him with those tiny licks. Only when his breath was uneven did she sit up slightly and use her hands to push her breasts closer together, creating the most wonderful, soft tunnel he had ever had the pleasure of burrowing into. He could feel her heartbeat gaining in speed as she stroked him. He strained to watch, turned on beyond belief at the view of her slumberous eyes, her moist parted lips. The pale globes of her breasts completely surrounded him, her pouty pink nipples almost meeting where his cock tunneled. He couldn't keep his eyes off that study in contrasts, her feminine beauty sandwiching his cock, flushed an angry red. He itched to reach down and fondle her round breasts while she pleasured him. Oh, she was good. She was perfect.

She watched his cock, drops of pre-come leaking from the tip, moistening her flesh. He shouted when she suddenly tilted her head down and swiped at the head of his penis with her tongue and then sucked it into her mouth. The world reduced to the drag of her flesh on his sensitive body, the warm wet suction of her mouth on just the tip when he emerged. "Yes. Oh, God." He started to thrust into her mouth, his balls tightened, his spine tingled, and then...nothing.

She sat up and freed him from the sensual prison, his crown releasing from her mouth with a pop. The back of her hand passed over lips wet from him. "So are you liking my fantasies now?"

It took him a moment to focus, his whole body geared up for an explosion. "Love them. Love them more if you'd let me finish. I'm begging you."

"Where's the fun in ending this quickly?" she purred. She straddled him, his neglected cock pointing up between her legs. Her hair tumbled down to her waist, the ends just brushing against his skin. She was flushed with arousal, her eyes hot with dazed hunger, her mouth silky smooth and wet. Her body glowed with health. She looked like a fertility goddess, and he was her welcome captive.

199

She distracted him from his musings when she reached down and deliberately spread her pussy, revealing the swollen little clit. She grasped his cock and he watched with fascination as she rubbed the tip against the nubbin. At the first pass, her head fell back and her hair lashed his thighs.

He jerked. "Genevieve. I've had enough. Fuck me."

She stopped moving against him, a satisfied smile playing over her lips. Genevieve leaned down close to whisper in his ear. "I can't tell you how happy I am you just gave me an order. Now I get to gag you."

He narrowed his eyes and his muscles tensed. "The hell you will." Fun and games were one thing, but he wasn't about to have a piece of cloth shoved into his mouth. He had never seen the appeal of silencing a partner when their screams of pleasure drove him higher.

"You'll like the way I silence you, I think." A careful tug of his earlobe made him shudder, and then she was sliding up his body in a graceful move until her breasts were even with his mouth. Never one to miss an opportunity, he drew her nipple within his mouth, loving the feel of her against his tongue. His hands curled, desperate to massage her breasts while he sucked her nipples, wanting nothing more than to give her as much pleasure as she gave him.

She pulled back from his mouth, panting for breath. "That's not what I was talking about." She moved further up his torso, before a flash of uncertainty darkened her gaze.

An inkling of what she wanted emerged in his brain and he almost whooped with glee while his cock hardened to a degree he had never experienced. Oh, yes, he was most definitely in love with a goddess. "Oh you sweet, sweet woman. Come on up here and sit on my face. And since that was an order, you have to silence me now."

Her skin reddened but she wore a determined expression. She threw a leg over his head, straddling his face and bracing herself with a hand on the headboard behind him. He had a moment to appreciate her rounded thighs on either side of him before he inhaled the sexual musk of her body.

Genevieve would never have thought it would be possible to be in such a position with a man and not feel horribly self-conscious, but the pleasure and intimacy scrubbed any lingering shyness away.

Alex nipped at her thighs before moving his mouth toward her vagina, the light curls providing no barrier to his determined lips and tongue. He worried her clitoris, making her shout with pleasure, before diving his tongue into her channel and setting up a rhythm that had her clutching the headboard and gasping along with him.

He turned his head to the side. "Rub your clit for me while I tongue you."

Genevieve ignored his rule-breaking and mindlessly obeyed, and he kept pace with the speed of her fingers with unerring accuracy. Her release burst upon her and she slumped over him. Every bone in her body felt like it had melted.

"Angel?" His voice was muffled, and she blushed, removing herself from his face so he could breathe, coming to rest in a kneel next to him.

She swallowed. "Yes?"

His body was strung so tight, he practically vibrated. "I know you like to rest after you come, but I really need some relief here. It's been too long. So since you're not a cruel goddess, can you please just climb on here and fuck me?"

Her body tingled anew at the sight of his penis, the ropy

veins heavily engorged. His fingers were clenched so tight around the frame of the bed that his knuckles had turned white. She straddled his hips and fumbled for his erection, directing it inside her. He grunted in appreciation and relief when he was fully sheathed, and then shouted in increasing pleasure with her movements as she bucked on his body. She came quickly this time, in a fiery burst. Alex ground his hips upward into her contractions, lifting her off the bed in his enthusiasm. She slumped over him again, out of breath, this time with the satisfaction of knowing she had pleased him too.

"That was awesome."

A lock of hair fell over his forehead and she brushed it back. "I'm glad you had fun," she said, smiling back. "You know, I am really good at taking control. I think I might have a future as a dominatrix. I saw this magazine once, and it had the most interesting toys…"

Alex groaned. "Stop. You'll kill me."

A loud ripping noise filled the room. She only had time to let out a single yelp of surprise before Alex wrapped his big arms around her and rolled her over, pressing her body into the mattress with the heavy weight of his own.

She gave him a mock glower and blew a piece of hair out of her face. "No fair. You could have gotten free whenever you wanted to."

"The fact that I didn't shows how much I liked it." He nuzzled her neck and stilled. Their hearts slowed together, beat together. "I love you, Genevieve."

She threaded her fingers through his hair, closing her eyes at the emotion and the huge bubble of happiness in her chest. "I…love you too." What a scary thing to tell someone. Hopefully, saying those three little words would get easier with practice, with security, with time.

Alex placed a loud, smacking kiss on her lips, breaking the seriousness of the moment. "My turn now. Assume position and get me some fresh scarves, woman."

She laughed, a joyous sound. "Make me."

Epilogue

Eighteen months later

Genevieve tooted the horn of her little used Honda as she rolled into the driveway of her and Alex's home.

She couldn't quite get enough of calling it their house. They'd bought the run-down two-story log home in the mid-sized Pennsylvania town almost seven months ago and worked hard to turn it into a cozy and comfortable retreat. She took a moment to admire it before climbing from the car. While she'd been busy with the home itself, Alex had turned the grounds into a showplace. Who knew, but she was living with quite the landscaper.

After popping the trunk of the car, she grabbed her backpack and used her key to enter. "Alex? I'm home."

Footsteps walked above her in their bedroom. "I'll be right down. How was class?"

"Good," she yelled back. "Hey, Diego, how's my little guy?" She rubbed the head of the big dog that had bounded up to greet her. Diego was still just a big ham of a puppy, who didn't understand quite what to do with his size.

After a few licks and woofs of pleasure, he went to go investigate the pattern of sun coming in through the window. Genevieve picked up the mail sitting on the foyer table. She rolled her eyes to discover it bereft of bills. When she and Alex had started living together, she'd been adamant that she'd pull her own share of their living expenses. Genevieve didn't want anyone to say she was mooching off him, and thanks to her frugal living for the past few years, she had a healthy bank balance. Unfortunately, if she didn't get to the mail fast enough, bills had a magical way of disappearing into space. When she asked about them, Alex would turn an innocent expression her way and suggest the mail nymph ate them. Then he'd start kissing her, and touching her, and pretty soon...

Genevieve sighed in fond remembrance and dropped her heavy backpack on the ground.

She had brought up the idea of starting a pre-med track at the local college a couple of months ago, to channel her abilities and interests into a more legitimate profession, and much to her delight, Alex had wholeheartedly championed her. She only had another semester to go before she could start applying to medical schools.

And she had to say, they had a lot of fun with the pair of pompoms she had picked up at the campus store.

Living with Alex was bliss in a lot of other ways as well. Their home was isolated enough that she wasn't overwhelmed by too many people. She had made enough good friends to keep her happy and busy. As for her old friends, Alex had a small barn built out back to keep Barney.

After quitting the police force in Harrison, he'd decided he wanted to try something different. An old friend told him about a start-up non-profit that helped teens who were recovering drug addicts. The job they'd offered seemed tailor-made for Alex's personality. The hours were flexible, the pay was decent, and he could get back to doing what he loved: feeling as if he was tangibly helping people. Lately, he'd been making noises about taking some classes himself to become a certified counselor. Genevieve approved, completely.

Thudding footsteps on the stairs behind her heralded his arrival, and she turned with a smile. Looking yummy in only a pair of jeans, his hair and chest still damp, he walked over to give her a lingering kiss.

"You're home early," he murmured against her lips.

Her arms crept up to wind around his neck. "Thought you might want to try out that new Jacuzzi."

"Mmmm, sounds good. The family's coming in tonight, though."

Genevieve smiled, loving the way he called his mother and brother "the family" or "their family" never just his family. What a family it was. Though Alex's immediate family was small, he had a slew of relatives. She'd met a virtual dizzying array of aunts, uncles and cousins over Christmas. They'd asked insanely nosy questions about Alex's and her relationship, where they'd met, and even when they could expect some kids. Genevieve had had the feeling she would have been lynched if she'd admitted she was on the pill. It had been awesome.

Alex's mother was a short, round little thing with a breathy voice, a tendency to hug, and a will of iron—necessary, she had confided in Genevieve, when dealing with the Rivera men. She and Christina had clicked instantly when they met.

Alex's brother, on the other hand...

Genevieve leaned back and eyed Alex suspiciously. "Is Linc going to ask me if I'm willing to sign a prenup again?"

Alex shrugged with a sheepish smile. "Maybe. But you can just offer to show him your bank statements again."

"Yeah. Only your brother would have insisted I actually produce them."

Alex chuckled and then held something out for her. "Here."

Genevieve accepted the envelope. "A-ha! I knew you got to the mail ahead of me. What's this?" It wasn't a bill, she realized, but a letter. The postmark read Puerto Rico.

"You remember my cousin?"

"Which one? After the first hundred, I started to lose track."

He smiled, but his gaze was watchful. "Maria. The one I told you about."

Ah. The midwife from Puerto Rico, the one who the others in the family regarded with awe. Yes, they'd met during the holiday festivities, and Genevieve had realized that Alex hadn't been lying. She hadn't needed to read the other young woman's aura to know she possessed power, probably on par with or more than Genevieve did.

The pretty woman had looked a bit stunned when she'd shaken Genevieve's hand, so she knew the surprise hadn't been on her side alone. "Why is it addressed to me?"

"'Cause I took her aside after she met you. I wanted to see if she could read your aura."

Genevieve blinked. "Could she?"

"Yup." He nodded at the envelope. "I asked her not to tell me, but to write down what she saw. You'll see I didn't read it. It's still sealed."

Sure enough, the back of the envelope was stuck tight, Maria's signature scrawled across the seal. "Why did you do that?"

"Because sometimes I see you thinking, and I know you're feeling like you still haven't done enough to make up for your supposed sins. I need you to forgive yourself completely, to believe that you're as good inside as you tell me I am. Otherwise, I don't know if we can take this next step."

She stared at him, feeling a bit like she'd stepped off a cliff.

"What next step?"

He took her hand. "Come outside for a minute. I want to show you something."

"What did you do?"

Alex's eyes widened in innocence. "Nothing." He led her through the downstairs to the back door and paused before sliding it open. "Close your eyes."

Genevieve complied, though the envelope was burning in her hand. He grasped her and led her outside a couple of steps. "Okay. Open."

She opened her eyes and promptly gasped, her hand covering her mouth.

The backyard had been transformed. Where before there had been only lawn, rosebushes had been planted everywhere. The more mature plants had already started to bloom, splashes of color releasing a heady fragrance. "I have the plans drawn up to put out a covered patio here. You can take a look at them and tell me what you think. That way we can sit out here and enjoy the flowers when they bloom."

She couldn't speak.

"Genevieve? You like them? I've read up on taking care of them, and I got seven of the hardiest varieties, and they seem like they should be impossible to kill. Seven's supposed to be a good number, right? I remember you saying something about it."

She managed to nod.

"Genevieve?" His voice was anxious now.

He staggered back only a step when she threw herself at him, and his arms came up in an automatic embrace. He chuckled. "I guess you like them."

She nodded against his chest.

"There's one more surprise." His voice sounded more cautious now, not his usual confident self. He disengaged from her arms, turned her around and nodded to the closest bush. Genevieve approached slowly, confused by the flash of white.

There, on a little picnic blanket, sat her old doll, gowned in a haphazardly made white silk dress. Alex cleared his throat behind her. "I framed the scrap of silk from your grandma's dress in a shadow box, but this is supposed to be symbolic. I have a lot of respect for my mom's sewing now, I'll tell you that much. She dumbed down the instructions for me, but even then it wasn't easy."

Genevieve traced the painstaking, uneven stitches. Tears threatened to fall from her eyes and she blinked rapidly.

He cleared his throat again. "I put the terrycloth dress in plastic. I figured you might want to hand them down someday. But now Betty Lou has a change of clothes."

And the battle with the tears was lost. They coursed down her cheeks.

"There's something else next to her." His voice was low.

She brushed aside a fold of silk to reveal a small black box. With shaking hands, she opened the lid to behold a simple diamond solitaire ring with two winking amethysts flanking either side.

"Genevieve? You haven't said anything since we came out here."

She pulled the ring out and placed it on her ring finger before she turned to look at him. She straightened to her full height and gripped the envelope in two hands, not even hesitating before she ripped it apart. "I don't need anyone to confirm that I'm pure enough for you. When I'm with you, I feel beautiful inside and out. That's good enough for me." Honestly, whether she was good enough for him or not, they were meant to be together.

He relaxed and nodded to her hand. "And the other?"

A smile beamed through her tears. "Yes."

About the Author

Alisha Rai has been enthralled with romance novels since she smuggled her first tattered Harlequin home from the library at the age of thirteen. A mild-mannered florist by day, she pens sexy, emotional contemporaries and paranormals by night.

After a lifetime spent bouncing around the States, she is content to call sunny South Florida home for now. When she's not reading or working, Alisha loves to hang out with her close-knit family. She happily lives in a chaotic house filled with clutter, laughter, good food, boisterous kids and very loud relatives.

Alisha loves to hear from her readers! You can send her an e-mail at alishawrites@gmail.com or visit her on the web at www.alisharai.com.

The best laid plans can come back to bite you in the ass...

Whatever It Takes
© *2009 Sydney Somers*
Spellbound, Book 3

Government Operative Gideon Bishop thrives on high-risk situations, but even his most volatile mission is nothing compared to coming face-to-face with his past. He's spent the last four years trying to forget Tate Calder and their scorching affair, but the only way to get the information he needs is to keep her close—and keep his hands off her. Because the only thing riskier than protecting a woman who insists on hiding the truth is giving in to the attraction that still crackles between them.

All Tate wants is a quiet holiday with zero interruptions from her family, and even fewer from the witches' council bent on recruiting her. Instead, she finds herself on the run from lethal mercenaries and the police with the one man she never expected to see again. To protect her family's secrets, she'll do whatever it takes to keep Gideon from learning the truth.

Even if it means risking her heart to seduce him—over and over again.

Warning: Adult language, skin-tingling forced intimacy, late-night office seductions, hot explicit sex between reunited lovers and graphic violence perpetrated by mercenaries, spies and occasionally by magic.

Available now in ebook and print from Samhain Publishing.

The higher she climbs, the harder he falls...

Bridging the Gap
© *2009 Annmarie McKenna*

Carter Malone is usually the first one to make tracks before a woman starts getting any ideas. Permanent relationships don't fit into his personal blueprint. Now, for the first time in his life, he's burning up the sheets with a woman who makes him think about something more permanent...like spending the night. But she's holding something back, something he can't quite pin down.

As a woman in a man's world, Ryan Cooper is used to wearing a target on her back—and hiding her vulnerabilities. She hasn't let anything, not even the ever-present threat of an epileptic seizure, stop her from working her butt off to get the foreman's job with her stepfather's construction company. Then she discovers the guy she's been dating—okay, having the hottest sex of her life with—is the architect who designed the building she'll be overseeing. The last thing she needs is anyone thinking she slept with Carter to get the job.

Or worse, feeling sorry for her.

Before the dust clears, things get a lot more complicated. The previous foreman's injury was no accident, and whoever caused it is taking aim—at the target on Ryan's back.

Warning: This book contains almost fully clothed sex with a little bit o' spanking on an OCD-clean desk inside a construction trailer, a rogue set of pencils that just won't take stay for an answer, and sweet loving in a tub.

Available now in ebook from Samhain Publishing.

They're craving something sweet. She likes it spicy.

Glutton for Pleasure
© *2009 Alisha Rai*

Devi Malik knows how to heat things up. She does it every night as head chef in her family's Indian restaurant. Her love life, though, is stuck in the subzero freezer. Now, with a chance to fulfill a secret fantasy with her long-time crush and his brother, it's time to put her desire on the front *two* burners.

For Marcus Callahan, a love-'em-and-leave-'em attitude isn't only a necessary evil of their kink. It's a protective device. Lately, though, his brother Jace has been making noises about craving something more.

Jace's dissatisfaction with their lifestyle grows with every glimpse of sweet little Devi. Yet Marcus is too haunted by the pain of their shared past to give love a chance.

Despite their reputation for vanishing with the dawn, they discover one night with Devi isn't nearly enough. And Devi finds herself falling in love with two very different men.

It'll take more than explosive sex to light up the shadows surrounding the Callahan brothers' secrets. But Devi's never been afraid of the dark…

Warning: This title contains two sizzling men for the price of one, ménage a trois, oral sex, anal sex, fun toys, great food, and creative uses for syrup and dressing rooms.

Available now in ebook and print from Samhain Publishing.

GREAT
CHEAP
FUN

Discover eBooks!

THE FASTEST WAY TO GET THE HOTTEST NAMES

Get your favorite authors on your favorite reader, long before they're out in print! Ebooks from Samhain go wherever you go, and work with whatever you carry—Palm, PDF, Mobi, and more.

Samhain
Publishing LTD

WWW.SAMHAINPUBLISHING.COM

CPSIA information can be obtained at www.ICGtesting.com
234985LV00001B/198/P

9 781605 047690